THE KING'S DAUGHTER OF DESTINY HAS THE KEYS TO HIS SECRET MYSTERY

JENNIFER THOMAS

ISBN   978-1-953821-66-9 Ebook
ISBN   978-1-953821-65-2 Paperback

The EC Publishing LLC books may be ordered
through booksellers or by contacting:

EC Publishing LLC
116 South Magnolia Ave.
Suite 3, Unit F
Ocala, FL 34471, USA
Direct Line: +1 (352) 644-6538
Fax: +1 (800) 483-1813
http://www.ecpublishingllc.com/

Ordering Information:
Quantity sales. Special discounts are available on quantity purchases by corporations, associations, and others. For details, contact the publisher at the address above.

Printed in the United States of America

TABLE OF CONTENTS

WALKING IN THE GIFTS OF DISCERNMENT, PROPHECY 1

THE PREDICTION FROM A METEOROLOGIST BROADCAST FORECAST A WEATHER REPORT 3

A SUDDENT MOVE SLAYING GIANTS IN THE DEMONIC REALM 6

EXPOSE TO A DEADLY INVISIBLE PLAGUE COULD THIS BE COV-19 PART #1 8

UNDERSTANDING THE POWER OF RESURRECTION VS OVERCOMING A DEADLY PANDEMIC 10

WATCH OUT FOR THE MARINE SEA CREATURES 13

THERES 8 PRACTICAL PRINCIPLES WILL CHANGE MANS COGNITIVE BEHAVIOR AND CONSCIOUSNESS LEVEL TOWARDS A MORAL VICTORY. 15

PROPHETIC NIGHT VISION, DREAMS AND ENCOUNTERS 17

THE DEATH ANGELS CAME KNOCKING ON MY DOOR POST Pt. 1 19

WHAT A WORD FROM THE PROPHET MOUTH 22

LAYING YOUR BURDENS DOWN AT THE ALTAR 24

BEHOLD A POWERFUL PROPHETIC ENCOUNTER 26

DALLAS TEXAS FURIOUS CATASTROPHIC ICE STORM 28

SARAH FINALLY BEAR'S CHILD 33

IRON SHARPENS IRON 36

IRON SHARPENS IRON 38

A TOMB STONE ROLLS BACK 40

THE PROPHETS VISION ALSO WRITE THE VISION 42

GOD'S MYSTERIES REBUKE THE STORM PEACE BE STILL 44

GOD HAS DECREED JUDGEMENT 46

C I A.. 48

HAPPY 55 BIRTHDAY JUNE 29, 2021 50

THE SON'S AND DAUGHTER'S OF ZION.................................. 51

MANIFESTING GOD'S LOVE GRACE, MERCY AND GLORY. 53

PRELUDE INTRODUCTION 55

DREAMING ABOUT LIONS TIGER'S WOLVES PART#1 58

THE DEATH ANGEL ARRIVED ONCE AGAIN WITH A
DEATH NOTICE PART# 1 59

THE COVENANT OF WEALTH.. 63

THE HOLY ANGELS SHOWED UP AND YESHUA
HAMASHIACH SHOWED OUT.. 64

WRITE THE VISION MAKETH PLAN 65

ADDRESSING A MESSAGE FOR CAPITAL HILL AND ALL
NATION'S. 66

A MYSTERIOUS PREMONITION OF DEATH ENCOUNTER
ONCE AGAIN 68

ANOTHER HOLY DIVINE HOOKUP 71

ESCAPING FROM EGYPT BABYLONIAN SYSTEM 73

THE HOUR HAS COME MINISTERING ANGELS
REVELATION.. 75

TOUCH THE HEM OF HIS GARMENT MIRCALES OF
HEALING... 77

MAN'S RAGING INTERNAL/WARFARE WITIN HIS OWN
MASS DESTRUCTION. 80

CRACKING COLD CASE MURDER MYSTERIES Pt. 2............. 82

CRACKING COLD CASE SPIRITUAL WARFARE MYSTRIES Pt.
2.. 88

WATCH OUT SIEGE FIRE AMBUSH ATTACK'S Pt. 2 92

TIME SEASON'S VS TIME ZONE'S 98

THE LAST DAY'S 102

A RANDOM ACT OF KINDNESS 104

TRANSMITTING CONNECTION THROUGH TELEPATIC TOUCH THOUGHTS.. 107
A MARRIAGE CEREMONY CELEBRATION THEN SUDDENLY DEATH OCCURRED Pt. 2.................................. 109
SEEING IN THE NATURAL VS SEE IN THE SUPERNATURAL 113
ORDER MY STEPS IN THY WORD....................................117
MEN'S HEARTS FAILING THEM FROM OUT OF FEAR........119
MAN'S MASTERING HIS OWN TOUGHTS WAYS CONDITION AND EMOTIONS BY SIMPLY NOT OBEYING GOD 121
DO YOU KNOW THE SECRET DNA SECURITY CODES?..... 123
AN APPROPRIATE APPOINTED TIME WHEN THRONS IN YOUR SIDES 124
BEHOLD WHAT IN THE WORLD IS GOING ON LORD...... 126
FLORIDA TROPICAL CYCLONE HURRICANE CATASTROPHICA DISASTER.................................... 128
THE LAST 444 FINAL CLARION CALL 131
BEHOLD WHAT IN THE WORLD IS GOING ON LORD Pt. 2 132
A PROPHECY AN PREDICTION FROM A FOUR-YEAR-OLD BABE WOW! 134
PHARAOH'S ARMY DESTROYED....................................136
REJECTED BY KINSMEN FOR HONORING MY GOD'S GIVEN GIFT'S AND SPIRITUAL GROWTH............................ 140
SEEKING GOD'S WISDOM IN PERILOUS TIME'S................. 143
SYNCHRONICITY NUMEROLOGY BIBLICAL PROPHECIES 147
THERE'S DEEP IMPARTATION FROM THE MOUTH OF A PROPHET 149
ANOTHER GENERATION CARRYING THE REVELATION . 151
ACKNOWLEDGMENTS 155
A BENDICTION 157
ABOUT THE AUTHOR..159

THE KING'S DAUGHTER OF DESTINY HAS
THE KEYS TO HIS SECRET MYSTERY

WALKING IN THE GIFTS OF DISCERNMENT, PROPHECY

I'AM A FORERUNNER AND PROPHETESS WHO CAN PICK UP ON DISCERNMENT EITHER GOOD OR EVIL MEANWHILE ON THIS PARTICULAR DAY JANUARY 23, 2019 THE HOLY SPIRIT GAVE ME INSTRUCTION TO GO FORETELL AND FOREWARN THE NURSES AND STAFF ABOUT ONE OF MY CLIENTS THIS SO HAPPEN TO BE AT A CONVALESCENT FACILITY SHE WAS SUPPOSED TO BE THERE JUST FOR A SHORT VISIT. BUT ON THIS VERY DAY I WENT TO GO VISIT HER NOW REMIND YOU THIS WOMEN WAS 95 YEARS OLD WHILE STANDING AND ATTENDING AT HER BED SIDE SHE WAS IN GREAT SPIRITS WE'RE COMMUNICATING LAUGHING ENJOYING EACH OTHERS PRESENCE MY VISIT STAY WAS FOR MORE THAN ONE HOUR IN A HALF MOREOVER THERE WAS TWO NURSES ASSITANTS WHO WERE PROVIDING HER WITH CARE. I THEN SUGGESTED TO BOTH OF THEM THAT WHILE SHES IN MY CARE AT HOME SHE SLEEPS IN A BED WITH SAFTY RAILS AT HOME SO THERFORE YOU MUST TRANSFER OR MOVE HER TO SOMETHING THAT PERHAPS WOULD BE SAFE AND SECURED NOW REMIND YOU THAT HOWEVER WAS MY FIRST SIGN INDICATION OF POSSIBLE DANGER I TRULY HAD FELT A UNPLEASANT SITUATION AT THIS VERY POINT SO MY VISIT ENDED WITH MY DEAR CLIENT WHILE HEADING OUT WALKING TOWARDS THE NURSES STATION ONCE AGAIN GIVING ADVANCE WARNING

OR NOTICE AND INSTRUCTIONS TO EITHER THE CREW OR STAFF MEMBERS WATCH OVER HER OR EITHER CHANGE THE BED FOR SAFETY PRECAUTIONS. WENT HOME THE VERY NEXT DAY I RECEIVE A PHONE CALL FROM MY CLIENT DAUGHTER STATING THAT HER MOTHER FELL TO HER DEATH OUT OF THAT BED THIS VERY TRAGEDY SHOULD'VE BEEN PREVENTABLE NO ONE DECIDED TO LOOK OUT FOR HER WELL BEING I WAS LITERALLY HEART BROKEN UNFORTUNATELY THIS INCIDENT COULD'VE BEING AVOIDED ONLY IF SOMEONE WOULD'VE LISTEN TO ARE TAKEN HEED TO THAT WARNING SIGN OF GODS VOICE. I'AM JUST A WILLING VESSEL SENDING FORTH THE MESSAGE WHO SO HAPPENS TO WORK IN A SUPERNATURAL REALM SHE WILL BE GREATLY MISSED I USED TO TELL HER IT WAS A HONOR AND PRIVILAGE AND PLEASURE WORKING ALONG BY HER BEDSIDE.

REST IN PEACE BELOVED
LULA MAE JONES
NOVEMBER 25, 1923 – JANUARY 29,2019

THE PREDICTION FROM A METEOROLOGIST BROADCAST FORECAST A WEATHER REPORT

ON THIS PARTICULAR DAY MARCH 03, 2019 WHILE GETTING PREPARED FOR CHURCH. NOW REMIND YOU I DIDN'T KNOW WHAT THE WEATHER FORECAST WAS GOING TO BE LIKE ON THIS DAY. THE ONLY THING I KNOW IS I GOT DRESSE HEADED, DASH OUT THE DOOR. I WAS WEARING A CREAM PAINTS DRESS SUIT WITH HIGH HEELS ON. NEXT AT THIS MOMENT I ENTER THE HIGHWAY THINKING NOTHING SO FARE AT THIS POINT I WOULD SAY THAT THE CHURCH IS APPROXIMATELY 30 MILES AWAY SUDDENTLY THE CLIMATE CHANGE DRASTICALY IT WAS POURING DOWN RAINING EXTREMELY WET AND COLD. HOWEVER, INSPITE OF ALL THAT EVENTUALLY; I BEGAN TO GO INTO BY SPEAKING, REBUKING PROPHESYING DELCARE DECREE PRAYING AND COMMANDING PLUS DEMANDING THAT WHICH THIS STORM TO BOW DOWN BEHAVE IN THE ALMIGHTY NAME OF JESUS CHRIST. LET'S PAUSE FOR A BREIF SECOND HERE NOW REMEMBER I DEFINITELY DID'NT HAVE A HEAVY JACKET NOR ANY RAIN BOOTS AND PERHAPS UMBRELLA I SPOKE EARNESTLY THESE VERY WORDS PEACE BE STILL UNTIL I COME FROM CHURCH AND THE LORD HEARD MY HUMBLE REQUEST SUPPLICATION AND PETITIONS DECREES, DECLARATIONS WERE SOON GRANTED WHAT SUCH AMIGHTY SUPER

POWERFUL MOVE BY OUR ALMIGHTY ABBA FATHER HANDS THAT WHICH HELD THE RAIN BACK SO YES I'AM TESTIFYING GIVING EVIDENCE AS A TRUE BELIVER AND A GREAT WITNESS MOROVER I WAS AMAZED AT AWE BESIDES FROM THAT THIS MOVE OR ACT OF GOD WAS EXTREMELY FASCINATING VERY INTERESTING I MIGHT SAY YESHUA HAMASHIACH IS STILL PERFORMING MIRACLES SIGNS HEALING AND WONDERS IN OUR WORLD TIME HISTORY ONLY IF WE CAN IMAGINE, IF HE DID IT FOR THE PROPHETS OF ANCIENT DAYS IN HISTORY ELIJAH WHOM HAPPENS TO BE ONE OF THE GREATIEST WELL ON THIS SPECIAL DAY GOD'S HAS SHOWEN ME THAT ANYTHING IS POSSIBLE ONLY TO THEM THAT BELIEVE IN THE WORD OF A TRUE LIVING GOD.

THAT STORM OBEY MY COMMANDS SIMPLY BECAUSE MY FATHER AND I BECOME ONE WHEN COMING INTO HARMONY AGREEMENTS. I'AM A NEWS WEATHER FORECAST, BROADCASTING THIS METEOROLOGIST RAIN PREDICTIONS AND REPORT ON TODAY STAY TUNE FOR THE NEXT REPORT.
"A SPOKEN WORD"

1 KING 17:1 AND ELIJAH THE TISHBITE, WHO WAS OF THE INHABITANTS OF GILEAD, SAID UNTO AHAB, AS THE LORD GOD OF ISRAEL LIVETH, BEFORE WHOM I STAND, THERE SHALL NOT BE DEW NOR RAIN THESE YEARS, BUT ACCORDING TO MY WORD.

MARK 4:39 WHEN JESUS WOKE UP, HE REBUKEDS THE WINDS AND SAID TO THE WAVES, SLIENCE BE STILL SUDDENLY THE WIND STOPPED, AN THERE WAS A GREAT CLAM.

I'AM JUST A WILLING VESSEL TRAIL BLAZER COME NOT TO ENTICE MANS EARS BUT TO DEMONSTRATE OR DISPLAY THIS DUNAMIS DYNAMIC SUPERPOWER TO CAUSE CHANGE AND AFFECT THE ATMOSPHERE. WE'RE TO BE INFLUENCER CHANGED AGENTS TO HELP BUILD GODS KINGDOM AND LIFT HIS HOLY NAME TO BE GLORIFIED. THERE'S POWER, POWER WONDEROUS WORKING AZUSA HOLY GHOST BAPTIZED FIRE.

A SUDDENT MOVE
SLAYING GIANTS IN THE
DEMONIC REALM

WHAT A WORD FROM BISHOP KENNETH C. ULMER WHILE ATTENDING CHURCH ON THIS DAY JULY 21, 2019 THE BISHOP PROPHESIED THAT SOMEONE WHO'S HERE TODAY WOULD ACTUALLY HAVE TO PACKUP AND MOVE SUDDENLY TO ANOTHER STATE WOW THIS WORD SHOCK ME AT AWE BECAUSE MONTHS PRIOR LEADING UP TO THIS DAY I WOULD ASK OR CONSULT WITH THE FATHER IF IT WOULD BE POSSIBLE LET IT BE THY WILL NOT MINES FOR ME TO GO TAKE CARE OF MY TWO GRANDDAUGHER'S. I FELT SUCH STRONGE URGE AND DESIRE SURELY REVELATION, CONFIRMATION TOUCH MY GREATER INTUITION AT THAT VERY MOMENT. I HAD MAYBE THREE TO FOUR CLIENTS THAT WHICH I WAS PROVIDING CARE FOR; SOTHEREFORE THE VERY NEXT MONTH ROSE AROUND AUGUST 24, 2019 I RECEIVED A PHONE CALL FROM MY OLDIEST DAUGHTER SHE WAS CRYING ASKING REQUESTING TO COME MOVE URGENTLY WITH HER AND THE TWO GIRLS THIS WAS DEFINITELY A SERIES OF A MATTER.

THE FULFILLMENT OF THIS PROPHESY CAME TO PASS HOWEVER; I HAD TO IMMEDIATELY TO ACTION BY PACKING IN SUCH A SHORT MOMENT NEVERTHELESS; GODS STILL SPEAKING TO HIS PEOPLE THIS WAS A DIVINE DECREED

AND ORDER ASSIGNMENT BEING HANDED DOWN OVER TO ME BUT ANY HOW LETS GET BACK TO WHAT I WAS SAYING MY STEPS WERE ORDER FOR THE RIGHT TIMING OF PROTECTION OR SAFETY OF THEIR WELL BEING SO YES DAUGHTER OF DESTINY MUST I REPEAT I MUST STAY IN THE THRONE ROOM OF PRAYER. WOW AND WOW! A SUDDENT MOVE SLAYING GIANTS IN THE SUPERNATURAL REALM I'AM GRATEFUL THANKFUL FOR GOD AND MY HOLY ANGELS WHO LEVEL UP WITH ME BY SLAYING THESE DARK DEMONIC EVIL FORCES THEY TRIED TO COME INVADE MY GRANDCHILD TREASURE BOX BUT THANKS BE THE GLORY OF A MIGHY KING WHOM I TRULY LOVE ADMIRED ADORED. I'AM CALLED TO CARRY THE MANTLE BREAK EVERY GENERATIONAL CURSES BREAKING CHAINS LOSING YOKES WITH THE POWER OF ANOINTING PULLING DOWN EVERY STRONG HOLD FROM A BEAST DRAGONS SNAKES LIONS WOLVES AND BIG FOOT THAT'S WALKING IN BETWEEN THIS EARTH CREEPING LURKING UPON THE FACE DEPTH OF THE SEA.

EXPOSE TO A DEADLY INVISIBLE PLAGUE COULD THIS BE COV-19 PART #1

ON THIS PARTICULAR DAY OCTOBER 25, 2019 WHILE AT A PHOTO SHOOT HANGING OUT WITH AN GROUP OF MODELS SOMETHING LEAP ON THE INSIDE OF ME. ONCE AGAIN SUDDENTLY WHEN IT WAS MY TURN TO GO UP AND POSE FOR THOSE PHOTOS SHOOTS MOREOVER THIS INDIVIDUAL WHO HAPPENS TO BE THE PHOTOGRAPHER THE HOLY SPIRIT QUICKLY GAVE ME A REVELATION ABOUT THIS PARTICULAR PERSON IT SAID THAT HE'S SICK SO I HOWEVER; IMMEDIATEY TOOK ACTION BY INTERCEEDING WITH SUPPLICATION PRAYING IN THE SPIRIT. WOW AND WOW! ITS LIKE DETECTING A PRESENCES OF SOMETHING UNUSUAL IN ADDITION THE HOLIEST INSTRUCTIONS WERE DOWNLOADING CONTINUE TO STAY AT THE ALTAR FOR THIS INDIVIDUAL FROM THIS POINT, WE AS BELIEVERS MUST STAY AT THE PLOW AND CONTINUED TO OBEY HIS COMMANDMENT. FINALY THE EVENING ENDED. WORDS CAN'T DESCRIBE MY FEELINGS RIGHT AT THIS POINT LOW AND BEHOLD SEVERAL MONTHS LATER I RECEIVED A PHONE CALL FROM THAT PHOTOGRAPHER BEST FRIEND AND THE NEWS REPORT WAS VERY SAD AND HEART BROKEN THAT SAME INDIVIDUAL PASSED AWAY ITS SUCH A HEAVY BURDEN UPON OUR HEARTS HE WAS ONLY 50 YRS YOUNG THE VERY CAUSE OF HIS DEATH WHICH UNFORTUNATELY

HE STRUGGLE TO RECOVER FROM PNEUMONIA I'M NOT TRYING TO SPECULATE THE DEATH NOR CAUSE OF THIS PERSON BUT THERES NO ACCIDENT NOR COINCIDENCE SOON AFTER THIS FATALITY DEVASTING DEATH THAT OCCURRED I'M JUST CONCERN WHEATHER OR NOT IF THIS INDIVIDUAL HAD COV19 BECAUSE NOT LONG AFTER I FELL SEVERELY ILL MYSELF. COULD THIS BE COV-19 EXPOSED TO THE ENTIRE WORLD A DEADLY INVISIBLE PLAGUE THIS EPISODE TO BE CONTINUED NEXT SEVERAL MONTHS LATER. Pt. 1

REST IN PEACE BELOVED

DANA SCOTT
JANUARY 19, 1969 - DECEMBER 9, 2019

UNDERSTANDING THE POWER OF RESURRECTION VS OVERCOMING A DEADLY PANDEMIC

A SLIENT KILLER WAS THIS THAT DEADLY PLAGUE? ON JANUARY 03, 2020

CALLED COV-19 I'VE BEING EXPOSED TO THIS FLU TYPE OF SYMPTOMS MY BODY WAS EXPERIENCING FEVER CHILLS COUGH SORE THROAT RUNNY OR STUFFY NOSE, DIFFICULTY BREATING EXTREMELY MUSCLE AND BODY ACHES, SUCH POUNDING HEADACHES. I THOUGH FOR A MOMENT WAS MY HEAD GOING TO EXPLODE I WAS TRULY TIRED AND EXHAUSTED FOR THE MOST PART. I'VE NEVER FELT SUCH LEVEL OF TRUMA NOR ANY IMPACT TO THE MIND, BODY AND SOUL HOWEVER I BEGIN PRAYING OUT TO OUR LORD RISEN SAVIOUR BY APPLYING THE WORD READING SCRIPTURES FOR HEALING. AT THIS POINT I FELT THAT I WAS GOING TO LITERALLY DIE KEEP STANDING ON HIS PROMISES SPEAKING LIFE EXISTENING TO RETURN BACK INTO A LIFELESS SITUATION MY NEXT STEP WAS TO PLEAD THE BLOOD THEN APPLYING THE HOLY ANOINTED OIL ALL OVER MY BODY MOREOVER AT ONE POINT I COULD'NT FUNCTION TO GET OUT THE BED WE MUST SPEAK TO THOSE UNCLEAN SPIRITS LIFE AND DEATH IS IN

THE POWER OF OUR TONGUES IN ADDITION TO THE STORY I EARNESTLY HAD TO STAY IN THE THRONE OF A PRAYER WARROOM FOR THE SAKE OF MY LIFE YOU TALKING ABOUT SOMEBODY PETITIONING REQUESTING, DECLARING AND DECREEING THAT THIS BODY BE RESURRECTED FROM THE DEAD. MEANWHILE I CONTINUED TO CALL OUT FATHER HAVE MERCY ON MY SOUL AND CAN THESE DRY BONES LIVE ALSO I ASK ABBA FATHER WHO WILL BRING ME A SLICE OF BREAD AND A GLASS OF WATER IN THIS DARKEST FINAL HOUR AFTER THAT REQUEST WHILE LYING IN A TOMB ON YOUR SICK BED OF AFFLICTION EXACTLY FOUR DAYS LATER PRAYERS AND SUPPLICATION WERE GRANTED I ROSE ONCE AGAIN WITH ALL POWER LET ME REPEAT THAT ONCE AGAIN I ROSE WITH ALL POWER. BOY OH! BOY THAT DEATH ANGEL CAME KNOCKING ON MY DOOR POST IT WAS NOTHING BUT THE PRECIOUS BLOOD WHICH SAVED ME OUR SAVIOUR REDEEMER AND HEALER, THANK YOU FATHER I APPLIED THAT OIL ON MY DOOR POST LIKE ALWAYS THERES POWER WONDEROUS WORKING POWERS FROM MY TOMB SAVED BY THE PRECIOUS LAMB WOW AN WOW! THAT DEATH ANGEL HAD TO BOW DOWN THANK GOD FOR OUR NURSE ANGELS WHO ARE EQUIPPED TO HELP TAKE ON EVERY BATTLE.

I'M STILL WONDERING, SPECULATING WHETHER OR NOT WAS THIS ONE OF THE DEADLIEST PLAGUE HAS CREEP UPON THE FACE OF OUR LAND THIS EPISODE TO BE CONTINUE STAY TUNE LATER STATISTICS DATA BASE SHOWS A STAGGERING ASTOUNDING REPORTS EXPLAINING MULTITUDE OF MASSIVE PEOPLE BY THE MILLIONS ARE BEING EFFECT OR IMPACTED THIS KILLER BEAST DEFINITELY A DEADLY INVISIBLE SILENT KILLER NEVERTHELESS THIS INVISIBLE SILENT DEMONIC PLAQUE ALL MOST SNATCH ME UNDER BUT GOD SPARE MY SOUL

I STILL HAVE LOST SOULS TO SAVE FURTHERMORE MY ASSIGNMENT IS GREATLY NEEDED PLUS GOD IS NOT THROUGH WITH ME YET. Pt. 2

"LISTEN TO A PARABLE"

JOHN 11:4 WHEN JESUS HEARD THAT, HE SAID, THIS SICKNESS IS NOT UNTO DEATH, BUT FOR THE GLORY OF GOD THAT THE SON OF GOD MIGHTY BE GLORIFIED THERE BY.

ISAIAH 53:5 BY HIS STRIPES WE ARE HEALED BUT HE WAS WOUNDED FOR OUR TRANSGRESSIONS, HE WAS BRUISED FOR OUR INIQUTIES THE CHASTISEMENT FOR OUR PEACE WAS UPON HIM AND BY HIS STRIPES.

WATCH OUT FOR THE
MARINE SEA CREATURES

ESCAPING THE WATER MARINE KINGDOM HELL'S DEATH TRAP ON THIS PARTICULAR SUNNY HOT DAY JULY 24, 2020

MY OLDEST DAUGHER AND TWO FRIENDS WERE OUT ON A BOAT AT A RESORT LOCATION ENJOYING THE WATER THEY ALL WERE EXCITED HAVING FUN. NIETHER ONE OF THEM WAS WEARING A LIFEGUARD VEST SUDDENLY THE HOLY SPIRIT MY GREATER INTIUTION RADAR ALERT ONCE AGAIN DANGER IS LURKING AROUND ABOUT MOREOVER I BEGAN IMMEDATELY WITH PRAYERS INTERCEEDING ON THE BEHALF OF ALL THREE YOUNG LADIES YOU TALKING ABOUT STANDING, PLEADING WITH ALL SUPPLICATION DECREEING WOW! I CALLED TO DISPATCH OUR PROTECTION GUARDING ANGELS WE STOOD IN AGREEMENT BY HELPING AND ASSISTING FURTHERMORE SLAYING THIS WATER KINGDOM BIG FOOTED BEAST OH! MY GOD THIS INDIVIDUAL I'AM REFERRING TO HIS PLOTS, PLANS OR MOTIVES WAS TO AIM HIS BOAT TOWARDS THEM WITH FULL SPEED AND EVERY EVIL INTENTION FORCE HE TRIED TO MAKE THEIR BOAT CAPSIZE LET'S PAUSE HERE FOR A SECOND NOW REMIND YOU THAT PREVIOUS WEEK IN THE NEWS HEADLINES THERE WAS UNUSUAL TRAGIC DEATH HAD OCCURRED THE VICTIM OF A YOUNG WOMAN WHO HAPPENS TO BE A MOVIE STAR ENTERTAINER HAD

LOST HER PRECIOUS LIFE IN THE MERCURY MUDDY RIVER WATERS I'M NOT TO SURE IF THE DIVER TEAM FOUND HER REMAINS I'VE GRIEVE AND MOURN THE LOST OF THAT PERSON LIFE. THE NEWS BROADCAST CHANNEL WAS ADVERTISING HER TRAGIC STORY WOW AND WOW! IT TOTALLY BLOW ME AWAY FOR SECOND THIS SAME INCIDENT COULD'VE TURN INTO A FATIAL HORRIBLE DEATH TRAP LIKE I MENTION THROUGH OUT TIME HISTORY I'AM A TRUE FIRM BELIEVER AND A POWERFUL PRAYER WARRIOR WHO HAS THE SUPERNATURAL POWERS AND ABILITIES TO SLAY GAINTS IN THE DARKNESS REMOTE PART OF THIS FOUR CORNERS AND REGIONS IN ADDITION ALWAYS BE CAUTIOUS STAY ALERT POST WARNING THERE'S DANGER LURKING IN A UNSEEN UNFAMILIAR WATER MARINE KINGDOM WORLD WATCH OUT PEOPLE THESE SPIRITS ARE SNATCHING BODIES UNDER THE DARK MUDDY MERCURY WATERS.

LISTEN TO A PARABLE

JOHN 10:27 MY SHEEP HEAR MY VOICE, AND I KNOW THEM, AND THEY FOLLOW ME.

THERES 8 PRACTICAL PRINCIPLES WILL CHANGE MANS COGNITIVE BEHAVIOR AND CONSCIOUSNESS LEVEL TOWARDS A MORAL VICTORY.

1. DEVELOP A MIND SET-THINK POSITIVE NOT NEGATIVE.

2. PINEAL GLAND-GIVES HUMANS THE MIND SKILLS TO COMMUNICATION, CONNECTING LOCATIONS THROUGH TRANSMITTING ELECTRICAL SIGNS PROCESSING PHOTORECEPTOR AND SNAPSHOOTS.

3. GREATER INTIUTION-GIVES A PERSON ABILITIES TO DISCERN GOOD OR EVIL BY EXPOSING MAN'S UNUSUAL BEHAVIOR AND MOTIVES.

4. PRECEPTION-REGARDING THE WAY OF UNDERSTANDING INTERPERTING MENTAL EXPRESSION TO THINK INSIDE OR RATHER OUTSIDE OF THE BOX.

5. CONSCIOUSNESS-BRING AWEARNESS TO CLEAR THOUGHTS BY BECOMING YOUR HIGHEST VERSION

EXPRESSING WHO I'AM MANIFESTING YESHUA HAMASHIACH.

6. SENSITIVITY TO LIGHT-IT BRINGS MORE EXPOSURE GIVEN YOU POWER, AUTHORITY TO OVERTHROW BY OVERCOMING YOUR FEAR FACTORS MANIFESTING THE DREAMS, GOALS AND VISIONS.

7. VIVID AND CLEAR- IT'S AN INTENSE FEELING THAT DOWNLOADING IMAGES OR SNEAK PREVIEW SNAP SHOTS IN YOUR PHOTOGRAPHIC MEMORIES.

8. INFINITE INTELLIGENCE-IS THE FORCE THAT GIVES ORDER AND ORIGIN TO EVERTHING IN THE ENTIRE UNIVERSE FURTHERMORE, YOU THE INDIVIDUAL ARE A PRECISE EXPRESSION OF THIS FORCE

A SPOKEN WORD

ROMANS 12:2 AND BE NOT CONFORMED TO THIS WORLD: BUT BE YE TRANSFORMED BY THE RENEWING OF YOUR MIND. THAT YE MAY PROVE WHAT IS THAT GOOD AND ACCEPTABLE, AND PERFECT, WILL OF GOD.

ROMANS 13:1 LET EVERY SOUL BE SUBJECT UNTO THE HIGHER POWERS. FOR THERE IS NO POWER BUT OF GOD. THE POWERS THAT BE ARE ORDAINED OF GOD.

SON'S AND DAUGHTER'S OF ZION YOU HOLD GREAT TRUTH VALUE TO OUR NATIONS, THERE'S TREASURES BUILD WITHIN THE SPIRIT MAN. THEREFORE GUARD YOUR HEART'S FOR OUT OF IT FLOWS THE ISSUES OF LIFE.

PROPHETIC NIGHT VISION, DREAMS AND ENCOUNTERS

WHILE ON VACATION MY DAUGHTER AND HER HUSBAND WERE IN THE STATE OF CHICAGO. LORD BEHOLD ON THIS PARTICULAR NIGHT OCTOBER 28, 2020 I HAD ENCOUNTER A PROPHETIC NIGHT VISITATION ABOUT THE TWO OF THEM WHILE STANDING INSIDE OF THE HOTEL ROOM DEBATING WITH ANOTHER PARTICULAR INDIVIDUAL THEY'LL WERE CONSIDERING THE POSSIBLITY RATHER THEY SHOULD LEAVE OR STAY THERE JUST FOR A FEW MORE DAYS I COULD ACTUALLY SEE THIS PERSON WHO HAPPENS TO BE A GOOD FRIEND OF MY SON-INLAW I'VE FOUND THAT NIGHT ENCOUNTER VERY QUIT INTERESTING WOW! IT'S AMAZING LOOKING THROUGH 2020 LENES FROM THE SUPREME POWER OF GOD. THE VERY NEXT DAY OR TWO WENT BY SUDDENLY THE PHONE RANGS THERE GOES MY DAUGHTER STARTED EXPLAINING IN FULL DETAILS DESCRIBING THE EVENT WHICH WAS TAKEN PLACE MOREOVER GOD'S DIVINE DOWNLOAD REVELATION SHOWED ME HOW THIS PERSON FEATURES WERE TO THE TOTAL EXACT PRECISE AND ACCURACY FURTHERMORE I WAS ABLE TO PICKUP TRACK THEIR CONVERSATION IT'S TOTALLY AMAZING, AWESOME TALENT OR GIFT TO CARRY. THE RADAR NAVIGATION SYSTEM STARED TRAVELING INTO TIME SPACE ZONES AND CERTAIN LOCATIONS ACROSS THE GLOBE PRETTY

IMPRESSIVE MAY I SAY, JUST ONE PUSH OF A BUTTON MAN'S STEPS SHALL BE PREORDAIN PREDESTINE BEFORE HAND LET'S PAUSE FOR JUST A SECOND HERE INADDITION I WOULD LIKE TO SHARE MORE INFORMATION THE TOTAL MAXIMUM DISTANCE BETWEEN NEVADA, AND CHICAGO IS APPROXIMATELY 1,747.5 MILES IF YOU CAN ONLY IMAGINE WOW! SUCH A TOTAL BLAST I'M WATCHING, STANDING AND NAVIGATING FROM THE THRONE ROOM SETTING IN GOD'S HEAVENLY PLACE. ONCE AGAIN THE SPIRIT MAN HAS TAP INTO THIS UNKNOWN SECERT WORLD IT'S LIKE AWAKENING THAT SLEEPING BEAUTY WITHIN YOU! WALKING IN HIS SUPREME POWER GIVES US ACCESS TO BECOME WITNESSES OF HIS AWESOMENESS MAGNIFICENT GLORY. I'M LITERALLY TALKING ABOUT GOD'S KINGDOM WORLD IT'S A REMARKABLE, MARVELOUS PHENOMENAL EXTRAORDINARY LIFE EXPERIENCES WHICH NO MAN ON THE FATE OF EARTH COULD EVERY GIVE YOU AND ME THIS RARE UNIQUE DISTINCTIVE GIFT ONLY BUT GOD.

THE DEATH ANGELS CAME KNOCKING ON MY DOOR POST Pt. 1

NIGHT VISITATIONS BAD SCRAY DREAMS ENCOUNTERS IN THE MID-NIGHT HOUR ON OCTOBER 30,2020 I HAD ANOTHER DIVINE DOWN-LOAD PROPHETIC PREMONITION REVELATION ABOUT MY SON THIS INDIVIDUAL CAME UP AGAINST MY CHILD. THE TWO OF THEM BEGIN FIGHTING ONE ANOTHER MY SON PLEADED WITH THE SUPECT TO DROP HIS WEAPON HE THEN FIRED HIS WEAPON IT DID'NT GO OFF SUDDENLY THE BULLETS WERE JAMMED INSIDE OF BULLET CHAMBER. THIS ENCOUNTER OCCURRED BETWEEN THE HOUR OF 3:40 AM I ARISE IMMEDIATELY OUT OF MY SLUMBER SLEEP BEGINNING TO SWIFTY START TAKEN ACTION CALL UPON MY ABBA FATHER AND THE HOLY ANGELS TO STAND IN A NEED OF A LIFE OR DEATH SITUTATION IT WAS CRITICAL NECESSARY FOR THE IMPORTANCE FOR MY OBEDIENCE TO BOW DOWN IN TOTAL SUBMISSION WITH EVERY PETITIONING, REQUEST PRAYERS, DECLARING DECREEING BY SLAYTING THE FORCES OF EVIL TO BOW DOWN WE MUST SPEAK OR PROPHESY COMING INTO ALIGNMENT AND AGREEDMENT TO CANCEL EVERY EVIL PLOT OR PLANS JUST PLEAD THE BLOOD OF THE PRECIOUS LAMB THE ALMIGHTY NAME OF JESUS CHRIST. I'AM A TRUE FIRM WITHINESS WE SERVE AND HAVE AMAZING FATHER DAUGHTER RELATIONSHIP

BESIDES FROM THAT I'VE UNCOMMON SUPERNATURAL FAVOR SUCH A DIVINE PROPHETIC POWERFUL GREATER CONNECTION NEVERTHELESS; GODS OFFICIAL ANSWER TO MY REQUEST AND SUPPLICATION ON THE BEHALF OF MY DEAR SON IT WAS NOT YOUR TIME NOR SEASON TO ACCEPT A PREMATURE DEATH CERTIFICATE GOD SO LOVE THE WORLD HE GIVEN EACH ONE OF US LEGAL RIGHTS POWER AND AUTHORITY TO SLAY EVERY DEMONIC ENTITY RATHER IT'S IN THE FIRST OR SECOND HEAVENS TRUTHFUL THIS BATTLE ACTUALLY BELONGS TO THE GREAT I'AM.

"LISTEN TO A PARABLE"

ROMANS 8:28 AND WE KNOW THAT ALL THINGS WORK TOGETHER FOR GOOD TO THEM THAT LOVE GOD, TO THEM WHO ARE THE CALLED ACCORDING TO HIS PURPOSE.

PSALMS 91:1-4-10-11

GODS WONDEROUS WORK HE THAT DWELLETH IN THE SECERT PLACE OF THE MOST HIGH SHALL ABIDE UNDER THE SHADOW OF THE ALMIGHTY.

91:4 HE SHALL COVER THEE WITH HIS FEATHERS, AND UNDER HIS WINGS SHALT THOU TRUST; HIS TRUTH SHALL BE THY SHIELD AND BUCKLER.

91:10 THERE SHALL NO EVIL BEFALL THEE, NEITHER SHALL ANY PLAGUE COME NIGH THY DWELLING.

91:11 FOR HE SHALL GIVE HIS ANGELS CHARGE OVER THEE, TO KEEP THEE IN ALL THY WAYS.

WHAT ARE THE THREE HEAVENS?

1. THE FIRST HEAVEN IS THE HEAVEN OF REALITY WE SEE WITH OUR NATURAL EYES.

2. THE SECOND HEAVEN IS WHERE SATAN HAS HIS THRONE AND THE FALLEN ANGELS DWELL UNHOLY DARK REALM.

3. THE THIRD HEAVENS IS WHERE GOD HAS HIS THRONE CELESTIAL KINGDOM AND RULES AND REIGNS OVER THE UNIVERSE.

WHAT A WORD FROM THE PROPHET MOUTH

MASTER PROPHET JORDAN ZOE MINISTRIES ON NOVEMBER 10, 2020

JENNIFER, NEW MILLIONAIRES ARE BEING MADE RIGHT NOW WILL YOU BE ONE

FEAR NOT, YOU BEASTS OF THE FIELD FOR THE PASTURES OF THE WILDERNESS ARE GREEN; THE TREE BEARS ITS FRUITS; THE FIG TREE AND VINE GIVE THEIR FULL YIELD: BE GLAD, O CHILDREN OF ZION AND REJOICE IN THE LORD YOUR GOD, FOR HE HAS GIVEN THE EARLY RAIN, AS BEFORE. THE THRESHING FLOORS SHALL BE FULL OF GRAIN; THE VATS SHALL OVERFLOW WITH WINE AND OIL. I WILL RESTORE TO YOU THE YEARS THAT THE SWARMING LOCUST HAS EATEN. THE HOPPER THE DESTROYER, AND THE CUTTER, MY GREAT ARMY, WHICH I SENT AMONG YOU. YOU SHALL EAT IN PLENTY AND BE SATISFIED AND PRAISE THE NAME OF THE LORD YOUR GOD, WHO HAS DEALT WONDEROUSLY WITH YOU. AND MY PEOPLE SHALL NEVER AGAIN BE PUT TO SHAME.

JOEL 2:22-26

IN THIS SEASON YOU'LL BE FIGHTING FAITH WITH A 2020 VISION POINT OF VIEW LET NOT THE TROUBLES

OVERWHELMED YOU WITH SO MUCH CARES OF THIS WORLD STAY FOCUS KEEP FIGHTING THE GOOD FIGHT OF FAITH TO UNDERSTAND THE HAND OF GOD IN THIS SEASON.

YE ARE MY BOLD COURAGEOUS LION'S

"A SPOKEN WORD"

1 TIMOTHY 6:12 FIGHT THE GOOD FIGHT OF FAITH, LAY HOLD ON ETERNAL LIFE, WHERE UNTO THOU ART ALSO CALLED, AND HAST PROFESSED A GOOD PROFESSION BEFORE MANY WITHNESSES.

LAYING YOUR BURDENS DOWN AT THE ALTAR

CONSULTING GOD IN THE MID-NIGHT HOUR BETWEEN 12:00 AM ON DECEMBER 16, 2020 I WENT BEFORE THE LORD REQUESTING FOR ALL GUIDENCE THROUGH MY EVERY DECISION MAKING AT THIS VERY POINT I WAS DECIDING HOW TO BRING ABOUT RESOLUTION WITH AN ISSUE I WAS FACING THE WINDOW TIME BETWEEN RECEIVING MY ANSWER WAS ONLY 24 HOUR LOOK AT THE HAND OF GOD MOVE SUDDENLY THE FOLLOWING NEXT DAY THE PHONE RINGS. AND THIS INDIVIDUAL HAD THE SAME EXACT ANSWERED I TRULY NEEDED AT THE FINAL HOUR MOMENTS SHE CALLED AT THE RIGHT TIME HOW PERFECT I'VE RECEIVED THAT IMPORTANT PIECE OF MESSAGE OH! MY GOD THIS PROJECT WAS AT IT'S FINAL STAGE TO PROCEED FORWARD INTO THE NEXT PHASE LET'S PAUSE FOR A MOMENT HERE NOW STAY WITH ME MOREOVER I'M SAYING THAT GOD GAVE THIS PERSON THE ANSWER TO HELP RESOLVE MY LIFE ISSUES OR PROBLEM. SO THEREFORE, WE'RE ABLE TO FINISH WHAT GOD STARTED IN A MATTER OF TIME NOW THAT'S WHAT WE WILL CALL A DIVINE DOWNLOAD REVELATION HOLY ANGELS HOOKUP FROM HEAVEN ABOVE.

TOUCHING THE HEM OF HIS GARMENT TAKE YOUR CARES, LIFE ISSUES ADDICTIONS AFFLICTIONS AND BURDENS TO

THE MASTER LEAVE ALL YOUR DEEPEST CONCERN TELL, THE LORD HE'S GLAD TO CARRY YOUR BURDENS HE WILL ALSO GIVE EACH ONE OF US THE DAILY STRENGHT TO HELP MAKE WISER OR BETTER SELF CONSCIOUSNESS IN OUR LABORING DECISION MAKING ALWAYS REMEMBER ONE THING A RIGHTEOUS MAN'S STEPS ARE ORDER BY THE LORD THE REIGHTEOUS CRY OUT, AND THE LORD HEARS AND DELIVERYS THEM OUT OF ALL THEIR PIT AT THE CROSS WE NEED NOT TO CONTINUE CARRYNG OUR BURDENS BECAUSE JESUS CHRIST HAS PAID THE PRICE FOR ALL HUMANITY, MANKIND SINS

WHAT A MIGHTY SUPREME SOVEREIGNTY REDEEMER WE SERVE, ADMIRE LOVE AND SHARE IN HIS SUFFERING RESSURECTION OF A TRUE DIVINE BEING IS WHO I'AM

"LISTEN TO A PARABLE"

PSALMS 55:22 CAST THY BURDEN UPON THE LORD, AND HE SHALL SUSTAIN THEE, HE SHALL NEVER SUFFER THE RIGHTEOUS TO BE MOVE.

BEHOLD A POWERFUL PROPHETIC ENCOUNTER

ON JANUARY 29, 2021

BEHOLD ONCE AGAIN ANOTHER DIVINE NIGHT VISITATION FROM THE HOLY ANGELS DOWNLOADING MESSAGES INTO THE SPIRIT MAN IV'E DREAMED ABOUT MY BABYSISTER FRIEND. THIS PARTICULAR PERSON LOOKED IDENTICAL TO WHAT I FORESEEN. I MEAN EXACTUALLY HER SAME COMPLEXION, HAIR COLOR LENGTH WOW AND WOW! REMIND YOU'LL I'VE NEVER SEEN THIS YOUNG LADY A DAY IN MY LIFE. BUT THOU OH! GOD

THE VERY NEXT DAY LOOK UP WHO ARRIVES MY SISTER AND HER FRIEND STOPS IN TO PAY MY DAUGHTER AND I A SHORT VISIT IT'S PRETTY IMPRESSIVE AND AMAZING LOOK HOW YESHUS HAMASHIACH SWIFLY SENDING A PROPHETIC POWEFUL DIVINE SPIRITUAL HOOKUP IN TIME ERA WITH SUPERNATRUAL CURRENT EVENTS STILL UNFOLDING CRACKING SECRETS CODES AND MYSTERIES IN WORLD HISTORY WHO DOES THAT ONLY TO THOSE ARE WILLING TO COME IN ORDER AND BOW TO THE KING OF KINGS AN LORD OF LORDS I COME TO BE A WITHNESS TESTIFY IN THE COURTS FROM A HEAVENLY THRONE ROOM ON EARTH SHOWING HOW POWERFUL NIGHT VISITATION, REVELATIONS ARE CONFIRMATION THAT

YOU'VE ALIGNMENT WITH THE GREAT CREATOR WITH ALL ASPECT.

GOODNESS GRACE AND MERCY SHALL FOLLOW THEE OUR DIVINE GUARDIAN ANGELIC ANGELS I KEEP SEEING NUMBERS 111, 222,333,444,555,777

888,757,11:11 HAVING THESE PARTICULAR SIGNS OR SYMBOLS ARE POWERFUL DYNAMIC AND SIGNIFICANT WORTHY TO PAY CLOSE ATTENTION.

HOWEVER. THIS AN INDICATION GOD'S HANDS IS UPON YOUR LIFE THERES A COMBINATION OR ATTRIBUTES AND VIBRATIONS WITH TOTAL LOVE PEACE, HARMONY.

WHAT IS A GUARDIAN ANGELIC ANGELS?

A SUPERNATURAL SPIRITUAL BEING WHO SERVES GOD MOREOVER ANGELIC ANGELS ARE CELESTIAL INTERMEDIARIES BETWEEN GOD AND HUMANITY INCLUDING THE ROLES BY EFFECTING AS A PROTECTORS AND GUIDES HUMANS LIFES, SOULS

BACK TO THE CREATOR WHO'S THE MASTER OVER THE UNIVERES MORE OFTEN BENEVOLENT AND SERVANTS ARE DEPICT AS ROLE, MODLES DEMONSTRATING DISPLAYING, REVEALING THE MARVELOUS GLORY OF GODS KINGDOM.

HOW DO I ACTIVATE THE MINISTRY OF ANGLES?

THEY WHO OBEY HIS WORD AND VOICE IT IN FAITH KNOWING THAT THEY ARE MINISTERING BEINGS SENT TO MINISTER TO YOU WHO ARE THE HEIRS OF SALVATION.

DALLAS TEXAS FURIOUS CATASTROPHIC ICE STORM

MY DAUGHTER, TWO GRANDDAUGHTER'S AND I FLEW TO DALLAS TEXAS FOR MY OLDEST GRANDDAUGHTER BIRTHDAY CELEBRATION PARTY FEBUARY 11-17 2021 LET'S REMIND YOU THIS VACATION GET AWAY WAS ONLY SUPPOSED TO LAST FIVE DAY'S STAY WITH THAT BEING SAID LET'S FAST FORWARD THIS FILM. THE VERY MOMENT WE TOUCH DOWN IT WAS EXTREMELY FREGIT COLD DAMP AND SNOWING, OUR URBER DRIVER FINALLY ARRIVED NEXT STEP WAS TO PICKUP THE RENTER CAR. AFTER THAT WE DROVE TO THE HILTON RESORTS HOTEL CHECK IN AT THIS VERY POINT WE'RE ALL SOME WHAT EXHAUSED FOR THE MOST PART DAY TWO GOOD MORNING AMERICA. WE ALL HEADED OUT ON A ROAD TRIP TO HOUSTON TEXAS TO GO EAT AT THIS GREAT FAMOUS RESTURANT CALLED TURKEY LEG HUT NONETHELESS, WHILE TRAVELING DOWN THE HWY THERE'S SNOW FLAKES FALLING WOW AND WOW! NOW REMIND YOU THERE'S A 4HOURS TRAVELING DISTANCE BETWEEN BOTH CITY. WE FINALLY ARRIVED AT OUR DESTINATION SAFELY THANKING GOD EVERY STEP OF THIS JOURNEY WE SUDDENLY PULLS UP THERE GOES A LONG LINE WITH MASSIVES OF PEOPLE STANDING WAITING TO ENTER. MY DAUGHTER GOT OUT OF THE CAR TO SEE ON LONG IS THE WAIT, WHICH WAS 2 INHALF HOUR WAIT; SOTHEREFORE WE DECIDED TO GO

ELSE WHERE TO HAVE BRUNCH. SEVERAL HOURS WENT BY WE PACK UP HEADED BACK TO DALLAS BOY OH BOY! SUCH TURKEY LEG HUNT. TRULY GIVING HONORS AND THANKS TO JESUS CHRIST THE KING OF KINGS FOR ALLOWING THE SNOW TO COME DOWN LIGHTLY BECAUSE THE ROADS CONDITIONS WERE SOME WHAT SLIPPERY. DAY THREE ROLES AROUND WE ALL PREPARED TO NAVIGATE OUT ON THE TOWN ONCE AGAIN THIS TIME WE WENT TO DALLAS WORLD AQUARIUM, WHAT A GLORIOUS MOMENT MY TWO GRAND BABIES WERE HAVING A STRIKING DELIGHTFUL MOMENT IN WATCHING DIFFERENT TYPES OF MAMMALS ANIMALS, LET'S MOVE ALONG NOW IT'S TIME FOR DINNER WE STOP OFF TO GRAB A BITE AT THIS RESTURANT CALLED PAPPADEAUX SEA FOOD KITCHEN. WOW AND WOW! SUCH GREAT FABULOUS HIGHLY DELICIOUS TASTEFUL FOOD. THE EVENING WAS SOON APPROACHING TO A END WE FINISHED OUR LOVELY CUISINE MEANWHILE HEADING BACK TO THE HOTEL BEHOLD SUDDENLY WE STUMBLE ACROSS A FATAL ACCIDENT THE MINUTE WE APPROACHED THAT SCENE IT TOUCH MY INNER MAN INTIUTION IMMEDIATELY I'VE FELT THE LOST OF SOMEONES LIFE IT'S A FEELING A VOID, VAGUE SENSE OF INSTINCTIVE POWER OF ENERGY RADIATING THROUGH THE VIBERATION IMPACTING ANOTHER HUMAN BEING SPIRIT. WE THEN SOON ARRIVED ONCE AGAIN AT OUR DESTENATION MOREOVER WHILE EVERYONE WAS PREPARING FOR BED MY DAUGHTER TURNS ON THE TELEVISION LORD BEHOLD BREAKING NEWS THIS NEWS ANCHOR MAN ANNOUNCING A YOUNG POLICE OFFICER TRAGIC DEATH HE WAS JUST SIMPLY DIRECTING TRAFFIC SO HAPPEN HE WAS STRUCK AND KILLED ON IMPACT WOW AND WOW! HIS DEATH TOUCH ME IT'S A UNUSUAL UNPLEASANT FEELING.

THE HAND OF GOD IS DEFINITELY TOUCHING, DEMONSTRATING THROUGH THE WORLD EVENTS WHICH DESCRIBING THE APOCALYPSE COMPLETE FINAL DESTRUCTION FROM THE BIBLICAL BOOK OF REVELATION THE IMPACT FROM THE ICE STORM HAS CAUSE MANY PEOPLE WHO WERE UNFORTUNATELY LIVING INSIDE OF THEIR VEHICLES FOUND STRAIGHT FROZEN TO DEATH NOT ONLY DID THIS WINTERY STORM HAD SUCH MAJOR IMPACT EFFECT THROUGH OUT PARTS OF THAT REGION HOWEVER DAYS PRIOR WAS A DEADLY ACCIDENT PERHAPS INCLUDING ONE HUNDRED CARS AND BIG RIGS TRUCKS PILE UP CRASH CAUSING SIX PEOPLE FATALITY, LET'S CONTINUE ON OUR JOURNEY DAY FOUR NOW THE NEWS BROADCAST AND LOCAL GOVERNOR DECLARES EMERGENCY DISASTER FOR THE STATE OF TEXAS. THIS ICE STORM TURNS INTO ONE OF THE DEADLIEST DEVASTATION CATASTROPHIC UNBELIEVABLE SNOW BLIZZARD IN TIME HISTORY.THE WHOLE STATE STARTED EXPERIENCING POWER ELECTRICITY SURGE ALSO FOOD WATER SHORAGE SUPPLY WERE LIMITED TO THE HOTEL GUESTS THIS EPISODE WENT ON FOR SEVERAL DAYS WE ALSO RECEIVED A TEXT MESSAGE ALERT THAT ALL AIRLINES FLIGHTS WERE CANCELLED, NOW EVERYTHING AROUND US STARTED TO OVERWHELMED AND CONSUME US LET'S REMIND YOU WE'RE SUPPOSED TO BE FLYING OUT TOMORROW EARLY MORNING WHICH HAPPENS TO BE THE FIFTH DAY. HOWEVER I IMMEDIATELY BEGIN PETITIONING DECLARING PRAYING PROPHESYING REBUKING THIS SNOW BLIZZARD TO CEASED STAY CALM IN THE MIST OF ALL THIS CHOAS PEACE BE STILL. KNEELING, PRAYING IN THE THRONE WARROOM WITH INTENSE PASSIONATE FERVANT HAVING DIALOGUE, DISCUSSION WITH MY ABBA FATHER AND HIS SON JESUS CHRIST AN THE HOLY SPIRITS NOT BUT LEASE THE GUARDIAN ANGELIC ANGELS. GOOD

MORNING AMERICA ON FEBUARY 15, 2021 I'VE ARISE EARLY AND THE SNOW SLOW DOWN WHAT AMAZING FEELING HE TOUCH ME WHILE EXPERIENCING THIS TANGIBLE BENEFITS BEHOLD THERE GOES THIS BEAUTIFUL SUNSHINE RADIATING ILLUMINATING, MOMENT I FELT A GREAT SENSATIONAL FEELING MY PETITION AND REQUEST TO THE KING WAS. IF WE SHALL FIND OR OBTAINED FAVOR IN HIS SIGHT BY NEVERTHELESS WE MUST ALL WAYS PRAY WITHOUT CEASING ON FEBUARY 16, 2021 ANOTHER DAY GOOD MORNING GODS PEOPLE I ROSE TO SEE GOD EYES SHINY UPON THEE CONTINUE TO KNEEL AT THE ALTAR SEEKING FOR AN ANSWER FROM OUR HEAVENLY FATHER. I'M STILL ANTICIPATING STAYING HUMBLE, GRATEFUL NOT COMPLAINING NOR MURMURING. NIGHTTIME FELL UPON THE DEEP REST AND SLEEP MY BELOVED DAUGHTER'S RISE AND SHINE DAUGHTERS OF DESTINY YOUR TIME HAS COME WE ALL AWAKEN ON FEBUARY 17, 2021 GLORY HALLELUJAH OUR ANSWER WAS GRANTED THE SNOW STORM AND GREAT WINDS CEASED AN THERE WAS A SENSE OF GREAT CALMNESS, PEACE FINALLY WE'RE ABLE TO PACK OUR LUGGAGES AND GO CATCH OUR FLIGHT BACK HOME.

"ELIJAH CRAZY FAITH"

2 CORINTHIANS 5:7 FOR WE WALK BY FAITH NOT BY SIGHT.

PRAYER
FOR WE LIVE BY FAITH, NOT BY SIGHT. FOR WE LIVE BY BELIEVING AND NOT BY SEEING. FOR WE WALK BY FAITH, NOT BY SIGHT. FOR WE WALK BY FAITH, NOT BY SIGHT.

MARK 11:22 AND JESUS ANSWERING SAITH UNTO THEM, HAVE FAITH IN GOD.

2 CHRONICLES 20:20 HAVE FAITH IN THE LORD YOUR GOD AND YOU WILL BE UPLIFTED; HAVE FAITH IN HIS PROPHETS AND YOU WILL BE SUCCESSFUL.

MARK 11:23 FOR VERILY I SAY UNTO YOU, THAT WHOSOEVER SHALL SAY UNTO THIS MOUNTAIN, BE THOU REMOVED, AND BE THOU CAST INTO THE SEA; AND SHALL NOT DOUBT IN HIS HEART BUT SHALL BELIEVE THAT THOSE THINGS WHICH HE SAITH SHALL COME TO PASS; HE SHALL HAVE WHAT SOEVER HE SAITH.

COMMAND, DEMAND START SPEAKING REBUKING PROPHESYING TO LIFES SITUATION CIRCUMSTANCES OR EVERY MOUNTAINS CEASED CALM THE STORMS PEACE BE STILL.

GOD KEEPS HIS PROMISES AND HE'S A PROMISE COMFORTER.

YE ARE MY WITHNESSES CALLED TO DUTY TO TAKE ACTION AND ACTIVATE THE POWER BY SHOWING MY INVISIBLE TANGIBLE SUPERNATURAL TOUCH WE'RE DEFINITELY LIVING IN SOME GREAT, CRAZY UNPRECEDENTED TIMES WHICH YOU AND I NEVER SEEN DONE OR CAN'T EVEN PHANTOM AND EXPERIENCES THESE SPECIAL MOMENTS, EVENTS ARE SUPPOSED TO BE RECOREDED FROM HIS GENERALS TO BECOME FIRST HAND WITHNESSES OF BIBLICAL PROPHECIES FULLFILLMENT IN THE 21ˢᵗ CENTURY TO GO DOWN IN WORLD HISTORY WE MUST BE ABOUT OUR FATHER'S BUSINESS AND MY BROTHER'S KEEPER GODS' ARMY STAY WATCHFUL CONTINUE TO PRAY.

SARAH FINALLY BEAR'S CHILD

BACK ON DECEMBER 24, 2020 ON THIS PARTICULAR DAY I HAD A DESIRE FOR PIZZA I HOWEVER DECIDED TO GO ORDER SOME PIZZA FROM MARCO'S MEAN WHILE THE WAITRESS STARTED TO TAKE MY ORDER SOON AFTER THAT WE BEGIN AN INFORMAL CONVERSATION OUR TOPIC WAS ESPECIALLY BASED ON THE TWO BOOKS I'VE PUBLISHED. BESIDES FROM THAT I MENTION TO HER MY STRONG BELIEFS AND WALKING BY FAITH NOT BY SIGHT THEN SUDDENLY SHE BEGAN MENTIONING AS A FIRM BELIEVER AS WELL. IN ADDITION TO THAT THIS YOUNG LADY STARTED DESCRIBING SOME INFERTILITY HEALTH ISSUES BETWEEN HER AND SIGNIFICANT OTHER THEY ARE UNABLE TO CONCEIVED WHAT THAT BEEN SAID MOREOVER THIS COUPLE HAS BEING TRYING FOR MANY YEARS TO BEAR CHILD. IMMEDIATELY WE STOOD IN PRAYER AND CAME INTO AGREEMENT LETS PAUSE THIS FILM JUST FOR A BRIEF MOMENT NOW STAY TUNE FOR THE NEXT EPISODE TO BE CONTINUED Pt. 1

BREAKING NEWS REPORT Pt. 2 TWO MONTHS LATER GUEST WHAT? THE UNTHINKABLE, INVISIBLE, TANGIBLE SUPERNATURAL TOUCH AND FAVORABLE OCCURRED ON FEBUARY 21, 2021 I WENT BACK TO ORDER SOME DELICIOUS PIZZA ONCE AGAIN TODAY SARAH CAME WITH SURPRISING BREAKING NEWS I'AM TELLING YOU BOY OH BOY! THIS

YOUNG LADY WAS EXPRESSING HER FEELING WITH GREAT EXCITING MOMENT DELIGHTFUL, OVER JOY SHE'S OFFICIALLY BEARING CHILD. WHAT A GREAT BEAUTIFUL WONDERFUL MIRACULOUS,REMARKABLE,INCREDIBLE TRUE TESTIMONY WHAT A TRUE HOLY GHOST FIRE DIVINE DOWNLOAD REVELATION HOOKUP THE CHILDRENS OF THE LIGHT MUST GO SHARE THEIR GIFTS BE A BLESSING TO THE WORLD LOOK HOW GOD CAN STILL BRING TWO AMAZING INDIVIDUALS WITH DIFFERENT CULTURES AND BACK GROUNDS WHICH HOWEVER IS REVELANT THROUGH GODS LENS WE DON'T SEE COLOR BARRIER WE HAVE NO ROOM FOR HATE, DISCRIMINATION WE MUST CONTINUE TO DISPLAY LOVE, LOOK AT OUR HEAVENLY FATHER WHERE IF TWO AGREED ON EARTH, HOW STRONG POWERFUL THAT WILL BE COME A FORCE THAT CAN'T BE RECKON.

"THE SPOKEN WORD"

GLORY, GLORY THERES WONDEROUS WORKING POWER IN THE NAME OF JESUS CHRIST OUR MESSIAH THE HOLY ANIONED ONE; WE SHALL CALL THIS BABY.

"THE GOLDEN CHILD"

MATTHEW 18:19 AGAIN I SAY UNTO YOU, THAT IF TWO OF YOU SHALL AGREE ON EARTH AS TOUCHING ANYTHING THAT THEY SHALL ASK, IT SHALL BE DONE FOR THEM OF MY FATHER WHICH IS IN HEAVEN.

MATTHEW 18:20 FOR WHERE TWO OR THREE ARE GATHERED TOGETTHER IN MY NAME, THERE AM I IN THE MIDST OF THEM.

HEBREWS 11:11 THROUGH FAITH ALSO SARAH HERSELF RECEIVED STRENGTHNTO CONCEIVE SEED, AND WAS DELIVERED OF A CHILD WHEN SHE WAS PAST AGE, BECAUSE SHE JUDGED HIM FAITHFUL WHO HAD PROMISED.

AMOS 3:3 CAN TWO WALK TOGETHER, EXCEPT THEY BE AGREED?
GODS PROMISES

HEBREWS 11:1 NOW FAITH IS THE SUBSTANCE OF THINGS HOPED FOR, THE EVIENCE OF THINGS NOT SEEN.

MARK 10:27 JESUS LOOKED AT THEM AND SAID, WITH MAN THIS IS IMPOSSIBLE; BUT NOT WITH GOD; ALL THINGS ARE POSSIBLE WITH GOD Pt. 2

IRON SHARPENS IRON

THE SPOKEN WORD FROM THE MOUTH OF PROPHET, BERNARD E JORDAN ON MARCH 10, 2021

JENNIFER DON'T ALLOW YOUR DREAMS TO DEMINSH! RESOLVE YOUR UNFINISHED BUSSINESS!

DEAR JENNIFER

"IN THE NEXT 30 DAYS OR LESS YOU'RE GOT UNFINISHED BUSSINESS TO RESOLVED JENNIFER AS YOU KNOW DURING THIS PROPHETIC REVIVAL, THE LORD DECLARED THAT12 MILLIONAIRES WILL BE MADE THIS YEAR THAT WILL BECOMING OUT OF HERE! YET, THERE IS SOME UNFINISHED BUSSINESS YOU MUST RESOLVE IF YOU DESIRE TO BE 1 OF THE 12 MILLIONIARES IN THE MAKING DO YOU BELIEVE YOU'RE WORTHY TO BE 1 OF THE 12? YES AND YES I AGREED

MOREOVER TO THE STORY HE MENTION ONCE AGAIN JENNIFER HOW URGENT IS YOUR FUTURE? THAT'S BECAUSE THE LORD HAS BEEN SHOWING ME SOME INCREDIBLE DEVELOPMENTS THAT ARE COMING INTO BEING! YOU WILL EITHER BE ON THE RIGHT SIDE OF HISTORY OR THE WRONG SIDE IF YOU DON'T RESOLVE SOME UNFINISHED BUSSINESS THAT'S TAKING PLACE IN YOUR LIFE? YES AND YES MAN OF GOD." Pt. 1

WHAT A POWERFUL PROPHETIC REVELATION

.

WHAT A POWERFUL PROPHETIC REVELATION

IRON SHARPENS IRON

ON THIS PARTICULAR DAY APRIL 6, 2021 I'VE RECEIVE ANOTHER PROPHETIC MESSAGE FROM MASTER JORDAN.

DEAR JENNIFER

IN THE WONDEROUS SPIRIT OF PENTECOST TODAY THE LORD TOLD ME TO TELL YOU THAT YOUR FUTURE IS THE MOVIE. IN WHICH YOU MUST PLAY EVERY ROLE! SEE WHEN YOU DREAM, YOU ARE THE ACTOR, THE PURPOSE THE AUTHOR AND THE DIRECTOR, YOU PLANE EVERY PART OF THE DREAM YOUR FUTURE IS THE MOVIE IN WHICH YOU PLAY EVERY ROLE. THE VILLAIN? THAT'S YOU, THE HERO YOU ALSO IN LIFE YOU ARE EVERY PART THAT YOU ARE PLAYING FRIEND FOE. ARE YOU READY TO STEP INTO THE ROLE OF YOUR DREAMS? YES JENNIFER, EVERY ROLE IN LIFE IS A PART YOU'RE PLAYING IN THE DREAM THAT EITHER BUILDING OR DESTROYING YOU'VE PLAYED THE ROLE OF THE VICTIM BEFORE, HAVE'NT YOU? YES AND YES YOU'VE EVEN PLAYED THE ROLE OF THE VICTOR, HAVE'NT YOU? YES IMAGINE PLAYING A PROPHETIC ROLE THAT'S COMPLETELY PURPOSEFUL TO THE FULFILLEDMENT OF YOUR FUTURE. ARE YOU PREPARED TO PLAY A CONSISTENT ROLE IN LIFE THAT ALLOWS YOU TO MANIFEST THE KIND OF FUTURE YOU SEE YOURSELF LIVING IN? YES TODAY YOU CAN PLAN TO PLAY THE PART CALLED I'M FORM HALLELUJAH. Pt. 2

"WELL INFORMED"

BY THE COMPANY OF MASTER BERNARD E. JORDAN

PROVERBS 27:17 IRON SHARPENETH IRON; SO A MAN SHARPENETH THE COUNTENANCE OF HIS FRIEND.

A TOMB STONE ROLLS BACK

HE HAS RISEN FROM THE TOMB LORD BEHOLD ON APRIL 09, 2021 I RECEIVED A ANOTHER NIGHT VISITATION ABOUT THIS CERTAIN INDIVIDUAL. MY SPIRIT MAN FORSEEN HIM WALKING DOWN THE ASILES AT WAL-MART STORE. LET'S REWIND THIS FILM FOR JUST A SECOND, IN ADDITION TO THE PERSON WHOM I'AM REFERRING TO WAS IN MISSING ACTION FOR QUIT SOME TIME. I WOULD APPROXIATELY SAY JUST OVER A MONTH IN HALF GOD PRESSED UPON MY HEART MY GREATER INTUITION PROMPT ME TO GET UP AND IMMEDIATELY START INTERCEEDING ON HIS BEHALF I'AM AN INTERCESSORY PRAYER WARRIOR THIS AN URGENCY WAR CRY IN THIS MID-NIGHT HOUR LET'S PAUSE THIS FILM FOR A MOMENT STAY TUNE THIS EPISODE TO BE CONTINUED Pt. 1

BREAKING NEWS REPORT Pt. 2 ONE MONTH PASSES BY HE SUDDENLY ROSE FORTH OUT OF HIS TOMB.

NEVERTHELESS WE ACTUALLY STUMBLED ACROSS EACH OTHER AT WAL-MART ON THE SAME ASILE I WALKED UP TO GENTLEMEN BEGAN EXPLAINING SIR GOD LAYED YOU UPON MY HEART THEN I SUDDENTLY WENT INTO THE THRONE WARROOM ON YOUR BEHALF HE THEN REPLIED AND SAID THAT HE WAS BATTLING SOME THREATENING CHRONIC HEALTH ISSUES.

STAY READY BE WATCHFUL THE HOURS HAS COME FOR GOD'S SON'S AND DAUGHTER'S OF ZION TO STAND BETWEEN THE MID-NIGHT CRIES.

A STUMBLING STONE ROLLS THEN LAZARUS ROSE FROM HIS TOMB.

THE PROPHETS VISION
ALSO WRITE THE VISION

IT'S PRETTY AMAZING A DIVINE DOWNLOAD REVELATION ANOTHER FILM ENCOUNTER WOW!

ON MAY 01, 2021 I'VE RECEIVED ANOTHER DREAM PERTAINING MOVIES BEING FILMED OR EITHER TO BE PRODUCED ONCE AGAIN THERE GOES 60 CREW MEMBER'S STANDING AT A CORNER. EVERYONE DRESSED IN ALL BLACK CARRYING THEIR FILM EQUIPMENT, IT APPEARD TO ME THAT THEY'RE WAITING TO BE ASSIGNED WHERE TO FILM THE PROJECT WOW AND WOW! HOW EXCITING HOWEVER I MUST CONTINUED TO WALK BY FAITH NOT BY SIGHT EXPECTING THE IMPOSSIBLE FOR WITH GOD BELIEVING ALL THINGS BECOME POSSIBLE. WRITE YOUR VISIONS FOR THE APPOINTED TIME AND SEASON SHALL REAP OR MANIFEST IN WELL DO SEASON IF WE DON'T FAINT DEATH IN LIFE IS IN THE POWER OF MAN'S TONGUES.

"LISTEN TO A PARABLE"

THE PROPHET'S VISIONS

HABAKKUK 2:2-3-4 AND THE LORD ANSWERED ME AND SAID, WRITE THE VISION, AND MAKE IT PLAIN UPON TABLES, THAT HE MAY RUN THAT READETH IT.

2:3 FOR THE VISION IS YET FOR AN APPOINTED TIME, BUT AT THE END IT SHALL SPEAK, AND NOT LIE: THOUGH IT TARRY, WAIT FOR IT; BECAUSE IT WILL SURELY COME. IT WILL NOT TARRY.

2:4 BEHOLD, HIS SOUL WHICH IS LIFTED UP IS NOT UPRIGHT IN HIM: BUT THE JUST SHALL LIVE BY HIS FAITH.

GOD SAID THAT YOU ALREADY HAVE LEAGAL RIGHTS AUTHORITY, DOMINION, AND POWER TO SPEAK THE PROPHETIC DECLARATIONS AND DECREES OVER YOURSELF INADDITON STAND BACK WITH GREAT PATIENTS BY OBSERVING HIS PROMISES AND YOUR PETITINIONS, PRAYERS, SUPPLICATIONS WHICH SHALL BE GRANTED MOREOVER WATCH THEM COME INTO FULL FRUITION; MAN'S OUTCOME OR RESULTS IS AFFECT BY MASTERING, MANIFESTING THE MIND OF GOD. STAY TUNE FOR THE NEXT EPISODE TO BE CONTINUE Pt. 1

GOD'S MYSTERIES REBUKE THE STORM PEACE BE STILL

A GREAT CEREMONY TAKEN PLACE ON TODAY MAY 21, 2021 WHAT A GREAT CEREMONY TO ATTEND, IT'S MY FIRST GRAND DAUGHTER GRADUATING FROM KINDERGARTEN. THE EVENT STARTS AT 9:30 am MEANWHILE THIS ELDELY LADY AND I BEGAN A CONVERSATION ABOUT WHAT CHURCH WE BOTH ATTEND AT FOR THE MOST PART ON THIS PARTICULAR DAY THE WEATHER IS VERY UNIQUE AN AWESOME QUITE A BIT CHILLY, SUNNY I SUDDENLY THEN WATCH INSTANTANEOUSLY HOW THE WEATHER CHANGE DRASTICALLY THOSE DARK GLOMMIE CLOUDS WERE HANGING OVER THE SKY FURTHERMORE FOR SOME ODD REASON MY GREATER INTIUTION KICK IN IMMEDIATELY I BEGAIN SPEAKING REBUKING PROPHESYING DECREEING DECLARING TO THAT STROM FOR IT TO SHIFT CHANGE MY PRAYERS REQUEST DEMANDING, COMMANDING THE STORM TO CEASE INSISTENTLY SEEKING GODS HANDS IN THIS GLOOMY DARK HOUR ESPECIALLY OBSERVING THE ATMOSPHERE SHIFTING INTO A OUT POURING OF RAIN I'AM GRATEFUL AND THANKFUL FOR GOD ALLOWING ME TO NOTICE NONETHELESS MAKE A QUICK DECISIONS AT THE RIGHT TIME WE WALK ACCORDING TO CLOUD BY DAY AND A PILLIAR OF FIRE BY NIGHT. IN THE DAY TIME HE ALSO LED THEM WITH A CLOUD, AND ALL THE NIGHT WITH A

LIGHT OF FIRE. THE CEREMONY WAS FINALLY OVER STAY TUNE FOR THE NEXT EPISODE TO BE CONTINUED

BREAKING NEWS REPORT AT THE TENTH HOUR APPROXIMATELY ONE IN HALF HOUR LATER UNEXPECTEDLY THE WINTER RAIN STORM APPEARS IN ADDITION THE RAIN CREEP UPON THE FACE OF EARTH THEN IT BEGAIN POURING EXTREMELY DOWN LIKE CATS AND DOGS WOW AND WOW! IT'S LIKE EXPERIENCING A HELL STORM.

WALKING INTO A NEW WORLD ORDER TIME OF MODERN DAY ERA. UNDERSTANDING LIFES TIME CURRENT EVENTS THE MYSTERIES AND KINGDOM LIVING HERE UPON EARTH THERES STILLS SOME GREAT TRUTH PHENOMENTAL REMARKABLE EVENTS TO CONTINUE TO RECORD IN MY LIFETIME OF WORLD HISTORY. THE PRAYERS OF THE RIGHTEOUS IS VERY POWERFUL AND EFFECTIVE

"A SPOKEN WORD"

"ELIJAH CRAZY FAITH"

1 KINGS 17:18
PSALM 78:14

GOD HAS DECREED JUDGEMENT

MAY 23, 2021

JUDGMENTS UPON THE PROUD LET GOD BE YOUR VINDICATOR

PSALMS 11:6-7 UPON THE WICKED HE SHALLRAIN SNARES FIRE AND BRIMSTONE, AND AN HORRIBLE TEMPEST; THIS SHALL BE THE PORTION OF THEIR CUP.

11:7 FOR THE LORD IS RIGHTEOUS, HE LOVES JUSTICE; THE UPRIGHT WILL SEE HIS FACE.

PSALMS 37:32 EVIL ONES SPY ON THE GODLY ONES, STALKING THEM TO FIND SOMETHING. THE WICKED WATCHETH THE RIGHTEOUS, AND SEEKETHNTO SLAY HIM THE LORD WILL'NT LEAVE HIM IN HIS HAND, NOR CONDEMN HIM WHEN HE IS JUDGED WAIT ON THE LORD.

ROMANS 12:19 BELOVED NEVER AVENGE YOURSELVES, BUT LEAVE IT TO THE WRATH OF GOD FOR IT IS WRITTEN, VENGEANCE IS MINE, I WILL REPAY SAYS THE LORD.

"MANS EVIL STATE"

JUSTICE JUDGMENT FOR GODS PEOPLE SAYS THE LORD ACCUSTED HOLD ON GODS FAITHFUL CHILDREN, JUST HOLD A LITTLE WHILE LONGER WE SHALL WITNESS AND EXPERIENCE THE GOODNESS OF THE ALMIGHTY FATHER, HIS GRACE IS SUFFICIENT FOR YOU. FOR MY POWER IS MADE IN WEAKNESS

PROVERBS 3:34 THIS MOST HATEFUL OF ALL SPIRITS MUST BE CORRECTED, OR YOU WILL BRING UPON YOURSELF GREAT PAIN AND BRING UPON YOUR CHILD THE JUDGMENT OF GOD.

PROVERBS NIV 3:34 HE MOCKS PROUD MOCKERS BUT SHOWS FAVOR TO THE HUMBLE AND OPPRESSED.

JUSTICE FOR THE POOR

CHOOSE LIFE OR DEATH

DEUTERONOMY 30:19 THIS DAY I CALL THE HEAVENS AND THE EARTH AS WITNESSES AGAINST YOU THAT I HAVE SET BEFORE YOU LIFE AND DEATH, BLESSINGS AND CURSES. NOW CHOOSE LIFE,

BUT I SAY TO YOU WHO HEAR, LOVE YOUR ENEMIES, DO GOOD TO THOSE WHO HATE YOU, BLESS THOSE WHO CURSE YOU PRAY FOR THOSE WHO ABUSE YOU.

WHO IS THE BLESSED PERSON IN THE BIBLE?

FROM A BIBLICAL POINT A VIEW, A BLESSED PERSON IS FIRST AND FOREMOST A MAN OR WOMAN WHO IS IN A RELATIONSHIP WITH GOD THROUGH JESUS CHRIST AND WHO NO LONGER SUBMITS TO THE WORLD BUT NOW SUBMITS TO THE WORD.

CIA

UNIVERSAL INFINITE INTELLIGENCE AGENTS

GOD'S WAYS ARE RIGHT
WE KNOW THAT GOD IS ALL-KNOWING.

1. OMNIPRESENCE- GOD IS EVERY WHERE AT ALL TIMES.

2. OMINPOTENCE- GOD IS ALL POWERFUL.

3. OMINISCIENT- THE STATE OF KNOWING EVERYTHING.

"CONSULT WITH GOD"

AS YOU DECLARE AND SEEK, SPEAK OVER YOUR LIFE, WE'RE PROPHESYING INTO OUR FUTURE WE'RE ALSO BEING GIVING THE POWER FAITH AN AUTHORITY TO CLEARLY SPECIFIED OR ESTIMATE

PREDICTING THNGS INTO EXISTENCE WHAT SO EVER YOU BELIEVE WILL OR SHALL HAPPEN

GOD'S UNIVERSAL INFINITE INTELLIGENCE LAW'S

WE'RE SUPPOSED TO NAVIGATE ACCORDING LIKE A MAP WHICH REFERS TO THE BIBLE C I A AGENTS

JUNE 06, 2021

WHAT IS A C I A?

1. C- CO CREATORS WHO'S CHOSEN, CALLED AND COMMISSION.

2. I- INFINITE INTELLIGENCE, TRAIL BLAZERS AND INNOVATORS.

3. A- AGENTS, AMBASSADOR WHO HAS, ABILITIES AMBITOUS TO BRING CHANGES AS WORLD AGENTS.

CO-CREATORS INFINITE INTELLIGENCE AGENTS

REPRESENTING, ORGANIZING, ESTABLISHING AN FOUNDATION BY BUILDING A KINGDOM ADVANCE SYSTEM TO SET PRINCIPLES, RULES AND STANDARDS IN ORDER; ALL WAYS REMEMBER IT'S A WORKING PROCESS.

"LAWS OF ACTION"

HAPPY 55 BIRTHDAY
JUNE 29, 2021

"DAUGHTER OF DESTINY"

TODAY I'VE TURN 55 YEARS YOUNG WOW AND WOW! FEELING FABULOUS, FANTASTIC AT PEACE WITHIN MYSELF BESIDES FROM THAT ON THIS DAY MY TWO BOOKS WERE SUPPOSED TO BE FEATURE AT THE LONDON EXHIBIT WORLD BOOK TOUR FAIR. INSPITE OF ALL OF LIFES SET BACKS DELAYS CALIMITY, FAMINES UNPRECEDENTED PANDEMIC AND OTHER LIFES CURRENT EVENTS ARE CONTINUING UNFOLDING BEFORE OUR VERY OWN EYES MILLIONS WERE DYING BEHIND THIS SILENT DEADLY PLAGUE CALLED COV-19. FURTHERMORE I'M STILL GRATEFUL AT PEACE GOD HAS GIVEN ME THE OPPORTUNITY AND PRIVILEGE TO GIVE THANKS AND HONOR TO THE MOST HIGH I COULD BE SLEEPING IN MY GRAVE. BUT THANKS BE TO GLORY I'M NOT COMPLAINING NOR MURMURING BECAUSE GOD HAS BEING GOOD MORE THEN GOOD TO ME EVEN WHEN I CAN'T HAVE MY WAY I STILL HAVE A SLICE OF BREAD, A GLASS OF WATER AND SHELTER WHAT MORE CAN YOU ASK FOR.

THE SON'S AND DAUGHTER'S OF ZION

UNDERSTANDING THE POWER BY WALKING IN YOUR GOD GIVEN KINGDOM AUTHORITY, ON THIS DAY JULY 23, 2021 CHILDREN OF THE MOST HIGH IF YOU WANT TO CAPTIVATE THE HEART OF GOD LISTEN ITS IMPARATIVE THAT WE MUST REPENT SUBMIT MOREOVER WE MUST ALSO REMOVE THE SCALES FROM OUR EYE'S AND GIVE ELOHIM AN ATTENTIVE EAR. SOTHEREFORE YOU CAN SHOW CASE HIS POWER OR EVIDENCE IN HIS PRESENCES. FURTHERMORE, BY WITNESSING, DEMONSTRATING WILL EITHER DETERMIND HOW MUCH LEVEL OF ENGERY THAT RESONATE THE GLORY BY DESTROYING DARK STRONG EVIL ENITIY FORCES. THE ANOINTING WILL BREAK EVERY CHAIN AND LOOSE THE YOKES JUST KNOW STAY READY FOR ALL TIMES FOR WARFARE BATTLES HOLD ON TO YOUR DREAMS OR VISIONS. THE CHILDREN OF ZION CONTINUE TO WORSHIP PRAISE AND REJOICE WHILE IN YOUR WILDERNESS SEASON OF CAPTIVITY BLESSED IS THE PEACE MAKERS THEY SHALL BE CALLED CHILDREN OF THE MOST HIGH.

"THE SET TIME OF THE LORD'S FAVOR"

PSALMS 102:13 THOU SHALT ARISE AND HAVE MERCUY UPON ZION; FOR THE TIME OF FAVOR HER, YEA THE SET TIME IS COME.

BEHOLD THE FATHER WILL DO A NEW THING

SAMUEL 2:8 HE RAISES THE POOR FROM THE DUST AND LIFTS THE NEEDY FROM THE ASH HEAP. HE SEATS THEM AMONG PRINCES AND BESTOWS ON THEM A THRONE OF HONOR. FOR THE FOUNDATIONS,YOU LIFT THE POOR, AND HOMELESS OUT OF THE GARBAGE DUMP AND GIVE THEM PLACES OF HONOR FROM A DUNGHILL HE LIFLETH UP THE NEEDY TO CAUSE THEM TO SIT WITH NOBLES, YEA.

JAMES 1:12 BLESSED IS THE MAN THAT ENDURETH TEMPTATION: FOR WHEN HE IS TRIED HE SHALL RECEIVE THE CROWN OF LIFE WHICH THE LORD HATH PROMISED TO THEM THAT LOVE HIM.

THE THINGS THAT GOD HAS PREPARED FOR THOSE WHO LOVES HIM THE PROMISES OF GOD TO GIVE US ETERNAL LIFE INSPIRES US TO CONTINUE SERVING HIM DESPITE OF THE MANY SUFFERINGS, PAIN AND TRAILS THAT WE EXPERIENCE A FATHER HEART IS TO GUIDE AND GUARD PROTECT THOSE WHOM HE CHASESIN AND LOVE.

PSALMS 32:28 I WILL INSTRUCT YOU AND TEACH YOU IN THE WAY YOU SHOULD GO; I WILL COUNSEL YOU WITH MY LOVING EYES ON YOU.

MANIFESTING GOD'S LOVE GRACE, MERCY AND GLORY.

THERE ARE TEN WAYS TO DEMONSTRATE GOD'S LOVE.

1. DISPLAY GOD'S LOVE BY HOSTING OTHERS OPENING UP YOUR HOME IS A DIRECT WAY THAT YOU CAN SHOW GOD'S LOVE TOWARDS OTHERS BY SERVING OTHERS AS WELL.

2. DISPLAY GOD'S LOVE BY COOKING A DELICIOUS MEAL FOR OTHERS.

3. DISPLAY GOD'S LOVE BY PROVIDING TRANSPORTATION ON THE BEHALF OF OTHERS.

4. DISPLAY GOD'S GLORY BY PUTTING A SMILE ON SOMEONES FACE.

5. DISPLAY GOD'S GLORY BY STOPPING IN TO VISIT THE SICK, LEAST SHUT IN.

6. DISPLAY GOD'S GLORY BY KNEELING OR STANDING IN THE WARROOM PETITIONING DECLARING, DECREEING ON THE BEHALF OF FAMILIES COMMUNITIES, REGIONS AND EVERY FOR CORNERS OF THE EARTH.

7. DISPLAY GOD'S LOVE THERE IS NO FEAR IN LOVE BUT, PERFECT LOVE CAST OUT FEAR. STOP ALL EVIL HATRED TOWARDS ALL MANKIND.

8. DISPLAY GOD'S LOVE SHOW A BROTHERLY LOVE WHICH REFERS AS AGAPE LOVE UNCONDITIONAL LOVE THAT TRANSCENDS AND PERSIST REGARDLESS OF CIRCUMSTANCE.

9. JOHN 3:16 FOR GOD SO LOVED THE WORLD, THAT HE GAVE HIS ONLY BEGOTTEN SON, THAT WHOSEVER BELIEVETH IN HIM SHOULD NOT PERISH, BUT HAVE EVERLASTING LIFE.

10. JOHN 3:17 FOR GOD SENT NOT HIS SON INTO THE WORLD TO CONDEMN THE WORLD; BUT THAT THE WORLD THROUGH HIM MIGHT BE SAVED.

"NOW THAT'S WHAT WE CALL LOVE"

NO MAN HAS NEVER REACH THIS LEVEL OF POWER THE AWESOMENESS, AMAZING ENDLESS LOVE CALLED JESUS CHRIST FROM NAZARETH YESHUA HAMASHIACH. INADDITIONALLY PUT AWAY ALL WEAPONS SUCH AS MALICIOUSLY GOSSIPING FALSELY SPREADING RUMORS MANIPULATION, DECEIVING OTHERS BY ASSASSINATING ONES CHARACTER OR EITHER REPUTATIONS.

PRELUDE INTRODUCTION

"FAITHFUL DYNAMICS SUPERHEROES"

PROVERBS 19:17 SHE EXTENDS HER HANDS TO THE NEEDY "WHOEVER IS KIND TO THE POOR LENDS TO THE, AND HE WILL REWARD THEM FOR WHAT THEY HAVE DONE."

"WALKING IN THE SPIRIT"

PROVERBS 22:9 THE GENEROUS WILL THEMSELVES BE BLESSED, FOR THEY SHARE THEIR FOOD WITH THE POOR.

PROVERBS 28:27 TELLS US THAT WHOEVER GIVES TO THE POOR WILL NOT WANT.

PROPHETS IN THE CAMP
THE PROPHET'S VISIONS
THE LORD HATH SPOKEN

NUMBERS 12:6 AND HE SAID, HEAR NOW MY WORDS:

IF THERE BE A PROPHET AMONG YOU I THE LORD WILL MAKE MYSELF KNOW UNTO HIM IN A VISION AND WILL SPEAK UNTO HIM IN A DREAM.

THE BOOK OF RUTH TELL THE EXTRAORDINARY STORY OF GOD'S FAITHFULNESS TO ISRAEL IN THE LIFE AND WORK OF THREE ORDINARY PEOPLE, NAOMI, RUTH, AND BOAZ.

AS THEY WORK THROUGH BOTH ECONOMIC HARDSHIP AND PROSPERITY WE SEE THE HAND OF GOD AT WORK MOST CLEARLY IN THEIR PROUCTIVE AGRICULTRUAL LABOR, GENEROUS RESPECTFUL INDIVIDUALS.

GOD WILL BE STOW HIS BLESSING OF PRODUCTIVITY THROUGH HUMAN LABOR.

LET'S TAKE A MOMENT TO REFLECT IN THE LIVES OF AN EXTRAORDINARY MODERN DAY RUTH NAME DAUGHTER OF DESTINY. MOREOVER TO THIS STORY SHE'S A HARD WORKER WITH SUCH A BACKGROIND OF HIGH VALUES WORK ETHICS DEMONSTRATING GODS HAND ON HER LIFE BY PERFORMING, ORCHESTRATING AT A HIGH DEGREE OR LEVEL OF SUPERNATURAL POWERS AN ABILITIES WITH CHARACTERS MORALS, FUNCTIONING AS A EXCELLENT ROLE MODEL, LEADERSHIP. SHE'S ALSO WILLING TO WORK ABOVE BEYOND TO WORK UNDER HARDSHIP. WHILE THE EXPERIENCING CHAOS, CALAMITY AND A WORLD WIND ECONOMIC GREAT DEPRESSION SYSTEM FALLEN IN GREAT RUINS DAUGHTER OF DESTINY IS A REMARKABLE ASTOUNDING RARE UNIQUE PRECIOUS COMMODITIES NOT ONLY EXCLUSIVELY TO SPECIFIC MARKETS PLACES. HOWEVER SHE'S MOST DEFINITELY A PEOPLE OF RARE DISTINCTION IN ADDITION DAUGHTER OF DESTINY IS STILL PLANTING SEEDS GRINDING, GLEANING IN THE FIELDS OF BARLEY WHEAT. NEVERTHELESS, SHES WELL DESERVED A SENSE OF ENTITLEMENT WITH THE PRIVILEGES OR SPECIAL TREATMENT TO COLLECT ALSO GAIN AN ECONOMICALLY PROFITABLE REWARDS FURTHERMORE THERE'S UNPRE-CEDENTED HISTORICAL MOMENT HAS ARRIVED FOR HER TO CROSS OVER ENTERING INTO A NEW ERA OF ABUNDANCE, DELIVERANCE AND KINGDOM EXPANSION, THIS IS WHAT YOU CALL THE LAWS OF FESTIVAL HARVEST

REAPING FROM THE FIRST FRUITS AND YOUR LABOUR, THE GIFTS YOU CARRY IS ON DEMAND IT'S LIKE WALKING IN THE FIELDS OF GOLD.

"THE THRONE OF HONORS"

BLESSED ARE THOSE WHO SERVE THE LORD FOR THEY WILL REAP THE FRUITS OF THEIR LABORS AT THE RIGHT APPOINTED TIME; FUTHERMORE MOST PROMINENT IN RANK, IMPORTANT, OR POSITION OF A MONARCH.

"LISTEN TO A PARABLE"

PROVERBS 18:16 "A MAN GIFT MAKES ROOM WERE DESIGNED TO BE KNOWN FOR IS YOUR GIFT. GOD HAS PUT A GIFT OR TALENT IN EVERY PERSON THAT THE WORLD WILL MAKE ROOM FOR."

DREAMING ABOUT LIONS TIGER'S WOLVES PART#1

IN THE MID-NIGHT HOUR I'VE ENCOUNTER ANOTHER PROPHETIC DREAM ON THIS DAY OCTOBER 24, 2021 THERE WERE SEVERAL TIGERS LIONS, WOLVES STANDING ALL AROUND ME. THEY KEPT ATTEMPTING TO CHARGE AT ME IT FELT LIKE THESE VICIOUS ANIMALS WANTED TO ATTACK. I SEEN ONE LIONS PAWS WERE BLEEDING WITH SO MUCH BLOOD. THEN SUDDENLY THE PACK OF CRUEL WILD BEASTS DISAPPEARED NOW REMIND YOU I AWAKEN EARLY THE VERY NEXT DAY BY PICKING UP MY PHONE SCROLLING THROUGH THE YOU TUBE CHANNELS BEGAN TO ADVERTIES LIONS, TIGERS AND WOLVES UPON EVERYONE'S CHANNELS ALL DAY NOW STAY WITH ME FOR A SECOND HERE. THE TOPIC THEME WAS BASED UPON INSPIRITIONAL ENCOURAGING SPOKEN WORDS BY PASTOR BISHOP MOTOIVATIONAL SPEAKERS TALKING AND DICUSSION ABOUT HOW BOLD, AND COURAGEOUS YOU MUST HOWEVER REMAIN BY STANDING, SLAYING PRAYING ON THE BATTLE FIELDS TAKEN POSITION SUBDUING RULING WITH A GREAT KINGDOMSHIP MIND SET TO REIGN AS AUTHORITY LEADERS BY NAVIGATING MOVING FORWARD INTO YOUR DESTINY; STAY TUNE FOR THE NEXT EPISODE TO BE CONTINUE.

THE DEATH ANGEL ARRIVED ONCE AGAIN WITH A DEATH NOTICE PART# 1

THE DEATH ANGEL INTENTIONS WAS TO COME THREATING BY SERVING A PREMATURE DEATH CERTIFICATE ON THIS PARTICULAR NIGHT OCTOBER 30, 2021 THAT EVIL DARK ENITIY FORCES COMES TO KILL STEAL DESTROY AND ATTACK YOUR PEACE OH YEAH!

LET ME REPEAT ONCE AGAIN THE DEATH ANGEL ARRIVED ONCE KNOCKING AT OUR DOOR POST. I PEEKED OUT THE PEEPHOLE BUT I DID'NT BOW DOWN TO THE ENEMY PLOTS OR PLANS BEHOLD ANOTHER SUPER-NATURAL DIVINE ENCOUNTER, THE HOLY OF HOLIEST WAS SHOWING ME A NIGHT VISITATION ABOUT THIS CERTAIN INDIVIDUAL STANDING OVER MY SON WITH AN FIREARM, FIRING MANY ROUNDS BUT SOME HOW NONE OF THE BULLETS HIT NOR PINETRATE MY CHILD BODY SUDDENLY I AWAKEN TO THIS DISTURBING HORRIBLE NIGHTMARE. MY NEXT STEP IMMEDATELY REACTION WAS TO TAKE FULL AUTHORITY BY CALLING UPON JESUS CHRIST, HOLY SPIRIT, AND MY PROTECTOR GUARDING ANGELS TO HELP LEVEL UP BY SLAYING THIS DEMONIC EVIL GAINT WITH REQUESTIN, PETITIONING PRAYING WARRIORING PLEADING THE BLOOD IN THE SPIRIT REALM TO DESTROY BY INTERRUPTING SATAN'S PLANS. GOD HAS DISPATCH HIS

HOLY ANGELS TO STAND AGREEMENT BY CASTING DOWN BREAKING EVERY GENERATIONAL CURSE WITH THE POWER OF ANOINTING WHICH LOOSE EVERY YOKES NOTHING BUT THE BLOOD SHALL PROTECT YOU WHILE SLAYING DEMONS DRAGONS TIGERSLIONS AND BEARS BETWEEN THE MID-NIGHT HOURS THERE'S A CRITICAL MOMENT OF WAR CRY TAKEN PLACE ITS EITHER LIFE OR DEATH. FINALLY AFTER THAT EPISODE THE VERY NEXT DAY I RECEIVED A PHONE CALL FROM MY SECOND DAUGHTER, SHE BEGAN QUESTION ME WHEN WAS THE LAST TIME I'VE SPOKEN TO MY SON. MY REPLY WAS I'VE NOT SPOKEN TO HIM LATELY I STARTED EXPLAINING TO HER WHAT TRANSPIRE THE PREVIOUS NIGHT I'VE RECEIVED A WARNING ALERT FROM OUR GUARDING ANGEL PERTAINING ABOUT THE SHOOTING OF YOUR BROTHER; LET'S PAUSE THIS FILM FOR A SECOND HERE STAY TUNE. LET'S CONTINUE THIS EPISODE HOWEVER THE NEXT SEVERAL DAYS PASSED BY MY SON SOON CONTACTS ME MY EXACT WORDS WAS SON YOUR MOTHER FORESEEN A HORIBLE SCRAY NIGHT MARE SUCH DEMONIC ENCOUNTER. MOREOVER I BEGAN DESCRIBING DETAILS BY DETAILS. I THEN PAUSED FOR A MINUTE HE BEGAIN EXPLAINING WHAT HAPPEN TO HIM THIS INDIVIDUAL APPROACH HIM WITH A GUN AND BEGAN SHOOTING CLOSE RANGE SURPRISINGLY SOME HOW THE BULLETS DID'NT PINETRATE NOR PIERCE OR PUNCTURE HIS BODY HOWEVER UNFORTUNATELY FOR THE PERSON WHO WAS WITH MY SON LOST THEIR LIFE, ONE OUT OF SIX ROUNDS PINETRATE AND PIERCE THEIR ARMOR I'M TRULY SADDENED FOR THE LOST OF SOMEONES ELSES CHILD. INADDITION THIS COLD CALCULUS PERPETRATOR ASSASSINATOR MUST BE FOUND AND PUNISHED AFTER A FAILED ATTEMP ON HIS LIFE NOT ONLY MY SON BUT FOR THE INNOCENT WHO DIED IN THE ARMS WHAT SUCH MERCILESS A HEINOUS ACT OF CRIME. WER'RE ALL SOME

WHAT EXPERIENCING SOME EMOTIONAL DISTURBING GRIEVING AND MOURING FROM THE LOST OF A DEAR LOVE ONE FRIEND DAUGHTER AND MOTHER. NEVERTHELESS WE'RE SURELY LIVING IN A TIME OF ERA NO ONE HAS RESPECT OR REGARDS TOWARDS GOD MAN HIMSELF NOR HIS NEIGHBORS THERES DEFINITELY SO MUCH ENVY VIOLENTS AND HATRED TOWARDS HUMANITY. THESE HORROR LOW VIBRATIONAL DARK ENITITY UNRESTED SPIRITS LURKING BY MULITPLYING INVADING THE STATES, COUNTRY AND REGIONS OUR WEAPONS OF MESS DISTRUCTION FOR TODAY IS KNEELING BEFOR GOD STAY IN THE WARROOM OH! MY GOD I'AM ONE OF GOD'S GREAT GENERAL WHO'S GIVEN PERMISSION TO SEE, HEAR, AND SPEAK PLUS CARRY THE MANTEL TO HELP DECODE UNFOLD SOME GREAT MYSTERIES PERHAPS CONVEYING A MESSAGE BY RECOGNIZING TO INTERPRET AND BARE WITNESS FROM THE SECOND HEAVENLY DIMENSION REALM WE MUST DISMANTAL THESE REGIONAL DEMONIC LEGIONS I'AM MAKING A DECLARATION AND DECREE TO OUR ABBA FATHER ALMIGHTY SOVEREIGNTY SUPREME GOD FURTHEMORE STANDING IN THE GAP PETITIONING REQUESTING TO FIND FAVOR I DAUGHTER OF DESTINY WILL OR SHALL PROPHESIED AND PREDICT ON THIS DAY THAT EACH PERPETRATORS OF THIS HORRIFIC CRIME MUST BE BROUGHT TO JUSTICE BASIS ON GOD'S KNOWLEDGE OR WISDOM AND REASONING TO PROPHESIED A FUTRUE EVENT IN THE CASE OF THE HOLY POWER TO HELP BRING JUSTICE FROM THE COURTS OF HEAVENS ON THEE BEHALF OF THIS FAMILY AND OTHERS FOR THEIR LOSSES AS WELL. STAY TUNE FOR THE NEXT EPISODE UNTIL JUSTICE HAS BEING SUCCESSFULLY PREVAILED.

IN SOCIETY TODAY IS IT WELL ACCEPTED OR IS IT WRONG FOR A PERSON TO KILL ANOTHER PERSON?

DOSE GOD SPEAKS TO HIS PEOPLE TODAY THROUGH THE GIFTS OF PROPHECY?

IN A GENERAL SENSE A PROPHET IS A PERSON WHO SPEAKS GOD'S TRUTH TO OTHERS SPIRITUAL WARFARE PRAYERS AGAINST DEMONIC POWERS & SANTANIC STRONG HOLDS.

"INSTRUCTION FOR WARFARE"

JAMES 5:16 PRAYER'S OF THE RIGHTEOUS PERSON IS POWERFUL AND EFFECTIVE.

"ACTS OF THE APOSTLES"

ACTS 1:8 BUT YE SHALL RECEIVE POWER AFTER THAT THE HOLY GHOST IS COME UPON YOU: AND YE SHALL BE WITNESSES UNTO ME BOTH IN JERUSALEM, AND IN ALL JUDEA AND IN SAMARIA, AND UNTO THE UTTERMOST PART OF THE EARTH.

"DAY'S OF PENTECOST"

ACTS 2:17 AND IT SHALL COME TO PASS IN THE LAST DAYS, SAITH GOD, I WILL POUR OUT OF MY SPIRIT UPON ALL FLESH: AND YOUR SONS AND YOUR DAUGHTERS SHALL PROPHESY, AND YOUR YOUNG MEN SHALL SEE VISIONS AND YOUR OLD MEN SHALL DREAM DREAMS:

ACTS 2:18 AND ON MY SERVANTS AND ON MY HAND MAIDENS I WILL POUR OUT IN THOSE DAYS OF MY SPIRIT; AND THEY SHALL PROPHESY:

ACTS 2:19 AND I WILL SHOW WONDERS IN HEAVEN ABOVE, AND SIGNS IN THE EARTH BENEATH; BLOOD, AND FIRE, AND VAPOUR OF SMOKE:

THE COVENANT OF WEALTH

SUDDENLY FINANCES WILL SHALL BE RELEASED BEHOLD I'VE RECEIVED ANOTHER DREAM ON THIS NIGHT NOVEMBER 09, 2021 IT WAS BASED ON CASHING CHECKS AT THE BANK, MOREOVER I WAS STANDING AT THE TELLERS WINDOW READY TO CASH THESE CHECKS THEN SUDDENLY TWO GUYS APPROACH THE TELLER WITH THEIR GUNS DRAWN READY TO TAKE ACTION BY ROBBING THE BANK IMMEDATLY I RAN OUTSIDE BEGAN TO TAKE COVER SAFETY BEHIND A REMOTE LOCATION. WOW AND WOW! WHAT VISION AND A SIGHT TO BEHOLD I'M GOING TO EXPLAIN THE MEANING OF AN ACCURATE REVELATION GUIDING INDIVIDUALS BY CONVEYING TRANSLATION WITH COMMUNICATION TO INTERPRET WAYS FROM THE SUPERNATURAL STAND POINT OF VIEW. MONEY GOD'S FAVOR SPIRITUAL AND NATURAL WEALTH, ALSO SPIRITUAL AUTHORITY, POWER MAN'S STENGTH OR GREED.

"A SPOKEN WORD"

IN THE BOOK OF DEUTERONOMY 8:18 YOU MAY SAY TO YOURSELF, MY POWER AND STRENGTH OF MY HANDS HAVE PRODUCED THIS WEALTH FOR ME. BUT REMEMBER THE LORD YOUR GOD, FOR IT IS HE WHO GIVES YOU THE ABILITY TO PRODUCE WEALTH, AND SO CONFIRMS HIS COVENANT, WHICH HE SWORE TO YOUR FOREFATHERS AS IT IS TODAY.

THE HOLY ANGELS SHOWED UP AND YESHUA HAMASHIACH SHOWED OUT.

HE'S STILL PERFORMING IN THIS HOUR BEHOLD ON THIS DAY NOVEMBER 24, 2021 THERE'S WAS A GREAT MIGHTY MARACULOUS MOVE OF YESHUA HAMASHIACH THIS PARTICULR DAY I PROCEEDED TO GO PAY A BILL. AS SOON AS I STEP FORWARD TO THE COUNTER THE SELLS REPRESENTER ASK HOW MAY I HELP YOU MY RESPONDS WAS I'M HERE TO PAY MY BILL THAT I OWE SHE THEN LOOKED INTO THE COMPUTER SYSTEM AND SAID MAMA! YOU OWE US NOTHING YOUR BILL HAS CURRENTLY BEING PAID UNTIL NEXT YEAR. INSPITE OF THAT NONETHELESS EVENTUALLY I BEGAN PRAISING GIVING THANKS TO OUR REDEEMER THE MESSIAH, BEHOLD LOOK AT WHAT HE HAS DONE IN THE SUPERNATURAL, BY UNFOLDING MANIFESTING INTO THE PHYSICAL OF REALITY THIS IS SHOWING EVIDENCE BY HIS LEVEL AND POWERFUL MIGHTY ACTS IN MY LIFE IN HIM WILL I TRUST GOD'S WONDERFUL HANDS WORKETH.

WRITE THE VISION MAKETH PLAN

ANOTHER ENCOUNTER ON DECEMBER 01, 2021 I'VE DREAMED ABOUT MEETING OPRAH WINFREY ONCE AGAIN THIS IS'NT THE FIRST VISION I HAD MANY ENCOUNTERS BESIDES FROM THAT WRITE THE VISION RUN WITH IT FOR DUE SEASON JUST HANG ON A LITTLE WHILE LONGER IT SHALL NOT LIE BUT COME TO PASS LET IT BE THY FATHER WILL NOT MINES JUST WAIT FOR THE APPOINTED TIME.

"LISTEN TO A PARABLE"

HABAKKUK 2:2-3-4 AND THE LORD ANSWERED ME AND SAID, WRITE THE VISION, AND MAKE IT PLAN UPON TABLES, THAT HE MAY RUN THAT READETH IT.

2:3 FOR THE VISION IS YET FOR AN APPOINTED TIME, BUT AT THE END IT SHALL SPEAK, AND NOT LIE; THROUGH IT TARRY, WAIT FOR IT; BECAUSE IT WILL SURELY COME IT WILL NOT TARRY.

2:4 BEHOLD, HIS SOUL WHICH IS LIFTED UP IS NOT UPRIGHT IN HIM: BUT THE JUST SHALL LIVE BY HIS FAITH.

AMOS 3:7 SURELY THE LORD GOD WILL DO NOTHING, BUT HE REVEALED HIS SECRET UNTO HIS SERVANTS THE PROPHETS.

ADDRESSING A MESSAGE FOR CAPITAL HILL AND ALL NATION'S.

A SPEECH TO OUR GLOBAL WORLD NATION'S ON THIS PARTICULAR DAY DECEMBER 12, 2021 I WAS PROMP BY THE SPIRIT MAN TO COME FORTELL, FOREWARN SHARE ALSO HELP BRING CHANGES ACROSS WORLD GLOBAL TO ALL HUMANITY.

HELLO WORLD I'AM DAUGHTER OF DESTINY HAS BEING COMMISSION ON ASSIGNMENT BY THE TRUTH AND LIVING GOD WHO I SERVE. IN TODAYS SOCIETY CULTURE WE'RE FACING SOME DEVASTATING CATASTROPHIC, CALAMITY ACROSS WORLD WIDE CURRENT EVENTS. THAT HAS BEING UNFOLDING BEFORE OUR VERY EYES HOWEVER WE'RE DEFINITELY REAPING THE WRATH BEHIND THIS DISRESPECTIFUL DISGRACEFUL STUBBORN REBELLIOUS STIFFNECKS GENERATION SOCIETY FURTHERMORE OUR PRESIDENT MR. JOE BIDEN MENTION ABOUT THE SOCIAL POLITICAL ENCONOMIC REFORM REPORT TO IMPROVE BUILD BACK BETTER INFRASTRUCTION PLANS. BUT WHAT MR. PRESIDENT DID'NT MENTION WE AS GROUP OUR A COLLECTIVELY AMERICAN CITIZENS MUST COME TO GRIPS AND TERMS BY UNDERSTANDING THAT IF WE DON'T I REPEAT IF WE DON'T TURN BACK THE HEARTS OF PEOPLE TOWARDS GOD. BY REPLACING HIS LAW'S TO IMPLEMENT

THOSE CAMMANDMENT BACK IN THE PUBLIC ARENA THIS IS A PLEA FROM DAUGHTER OF DESTINY STANDING IN THIS HOUR WITH A WAR CRY FOR CHANGE TO TAKE PLACE ON THE BEHALF OF MY BROTHER'S AND SISTER'S LET'S IMBRACE EACH ONE WITH LOVE, PEACE, HARMONY UNITY AND JUSTICE FOR ALL.

A MYSTERIOUS PREMONITION OF DEATH ENCOUNTER ONCE AGAIN

PREMONITION OF DEATH STRIKES IN THE MID-NIGHT HOUR ON THIS DAY DECEMBER 25, 2021 BEHOLD SUDDENLY HOWEVER I WAS STRUCK UNEXPECTEDLY WITH A HORRIFIED, SCRAY VISION I STOOD OUTSIDE OF THE CHURCH OBSERVING THE DEATH OF MY BROTHER IN-LAW LYING INSIDE HIS CASKET. I'VE RECEIVE A STRONG FEELING THAT SOMETHING WAS ABOUT TO HAPPEN. MY GREATER INTIUTION LEAP INSIDE THE SPIRIT MAN ESPECIALLY WITNESSING THIS UNPLEASANT INSIGHT. NEVERTHELESS I IMMEDATELY AWAKEN PROCEEDING INTO CALLING ON JESUS CHRIST, HOLY GUARDIAN ANGELS TO HELP REBUKE AND CANCEL THIS AWFUL BAD DREADFUL UNHAPPINESS MOMENT I SERIOUSLY STARTED CRYING NO JESUS NO THEN BEGAIN STANDING IN THE GAP PLEADING GOD'S BLOOD GRACE AND MERCY UPON THE PERSON THAT HIS SOUL WOULD BE SPARED IN THIS FINAL HOUR LET IT BE THY WILL O LORD NOT MY WILL. STAY TUNE FOR THE NEXT EPISODE TO BE CONTINUE. Pt. 1

BREAKING NEW'S THE HOLY SPIRIT CAME TO MY BEDSIDE AND DOWNLOADED THIS MESSAGE ON THE VERY NEXT NIGHT WHICH IS DECEMBER 26, 2021 ANOTHER SURPRISING SEQUENCE OF EVENT UNFOLDING THIS MYSTERY

HOWEVER I'VE RECEIVED A VISION ABOUT MY BROTHER IN-LAW WIFE, THIS TIME SHE WAS ACTING VERY STRANGE UNSETTLING OR HARD TO UNDERSTAND DUE TO HER HOSTEL BEHAVIOR TOWARDS EVERYONE.

PREMONITIONS, DREAMS VISIONS THAT PERHAPS COME TO US UPON OUR BED POST TO CONVEY AND TRANSPORTING MESSAGES BY GOD TO FOREWARN US GIVEN FIRSTHAND INSIGHT IF MAN- CONSCIOUSNESS STATE OF MIND SO WILLING AND ABLE TO CONCIEVE IT.

RECOGNIZING THAT GOD'S CONVEYING A PROPHETIC MESSAGE PRECOGNITIVE EXPERIENCE OR VISIONS SERVES AS A GUIDE AND TRANSPORTING THAT HOWEVER CAN BE USED TO PROVIDE A SENSE OF PURPOSE BY DEMONSTRATING DISPLAYING SUCH POWER OF MAN'S IMAGINATION WHEN YOU APPLY A PANORAMIC IMAGE TO SOMEONE'S FURTURE EVENTS. WILL CREAT OF FORM BLACK AND WHITE, COLOR PICTURES THAT CONSIDER MAN'S WAY'S EXPRESSING HIS UNIQUENESS DISTINCTIVE EXHIBITION INSIGHT AS A LIGHT REFLECTION OF THE MOST HIGH.

THERE'S A BIBLICAL INTERPRETATION MEANING OF DEATH IN A DREAM, OR A DEAD PERSON MIGHT ALSO MEAN YOU WILL OVER COME DIFFICULTIES IN YOUR LIFE.

CONSULT WITH GOD CONCERING ABOUT THE HEART OF ALL MATTER'S PERTAINING TO ANY DREAMS OR VISIONS RATHER IT'S GOOD OR EVIL NIGHT MARES BY ALL MEANS NECESSARY TAKE IT TO THE ALTAR, WITH SUPPLICATIONS REQUEST SEEKING ON WAY'S HOW TO UNFOLD OR DECODE THE NIGHT PROVISIONS ARE ENCOUNTER'S BY UNDERSTANDING TO CANCEL ALL EVIL ACTIVITIES AGAINST YOU. LIFE'S MYSTICAL SECRETS HIDDEN

CODES BEHIND OR BEYOND MAN'S CONSCIOUSNESS OR IMGAINATION CONDITIONING YOUR MINDS AS ONENESS GOD'S WISDOM AND THOUGHTS

"LISTEN TO A PARABLE"
MATTHEW 6:33 SEEK YE FIRST AND YOU SHALL FIND

MATTHEW 7:7 ASK, AND IT SHALL BE GAVEN YOU; SEEK AND YE SHALL FIND; KNOCK, AND IT SHALL BE OPENED UNTO YOU:

JOB 33:15-16 IN A DREAM, IN A VISION OF NIGHT, WHEN DEEP SLEEP FALLETH UPON MEN, IN SLUMBERING UPON THE BED.

33:16 THEN HE OPENETH THE EARS OF MEN, AND SEALETH THEIR INSTRUCTION.

"CROSSING OVER INTO PASSOVER"
SEASON'S

"THE YEAR OF 5782 BIBLICAL TIME"
SEASON'S

ANOTHER HOLY
DIVINE HOOKUP

WHAT A MIGHTY MIRACULOUS TOUCH I WENT TO THE DMV ON THIS PATICULAR DAY DECEMBER 27, 2021 BEHOLD SUDDENLY I DISPATCHED THE HOLY ANGELS TO GO BEFORE ME GUEST WHAT? THEY SHOWED UP WHILE THE LION TRIBE OF JUDAH SHOWED OUT HOWEVER I WAS SCHEDULE TO TAKE THE TEST EXAMINE TODAY I THEN PROCEEDED TO THE WINDOW. NEXT STEP THE CLERK ASSISTANCE BEGIN TO ASK FOR MY IMPORANT DOCUMENTS FURTHERMORE SHE STARTED INPUTTING THE DATA INFORMATION INTO COMPUTER SYSTEM. HER RESPONSE WAS MS. THOMAS YOU DON'T HAVE TO TAKE THE WRITTEN EXAMINE, I QUICKLY REPLY BACK ARE YOU SURE. SHE SAIDE YES SIMPLY ALL I NEEDED WAS $38.00 BUCKS AND TAKE A PHOTO PICTURE. I'AM TRULY GRATEFUL AT THIS MOMENT OUR FATHER IS DEFINITELY SHOWING HIS MIGHTY HANDS ORCHESTRATING UPON THE LIVES OF A TRUE FOLLOWER AND BELIEVERS INADDITION HE WILL THEN PUT THE EXTRA ON YOUR ORDINARY IT'S SUCH AMAZING GLORIOUS, REMARKABLE DIVINE POWERFUL SUPERNATURAL ACT ONLY FROM THE KING OF KING'S

IT AMAZED ME HALLELUJAH MIRACLES SIGNS HEALING AND WONDERS ARE STILL BEING PERFORMED IN THIS VERY HOUR IN TIME HISTORY.

THE CHILDREN OF GOD WALKING IN THE SPIRIT I WILL GO BEFORE THEE AND MAKE THE CROOKED PLACES STRAIGHT DON'T LEAN IN YOUR OWN UNDERSTANDING WHEN SOME THINGS DOES'NT MAKE SENSE JUST SAY YES LORD. WALKING DOWN THAT NARROW PATH WILL GUIDE YOUR SPIRIT MAN INTO HIS MARVELOUS SPLENDID KINGDOM WORLD IT'S SURPRISING, ASTONISHING, EXCITING AND A WONDER TO MY SOUL.

"A FAITHFUL SOLIDER"

ESCAPING FROM EGYPT
BABYLONIAN SYSTEM

IT WAS LIKE THE WHOLE WIDE WORLD OF BABYLONIAN SYSTEM FALLEN APART ON JANUARY 13, 2022 THERE'S HELL AND BRIMSTONES CONSUMING THEE IT LETERALLY FELT LIKE YOU WERE CAST INTO A FIERY FURNACE MOREOVER THEIR EVIL PLOTS AGAINST THE SON'S AND DAUGHTER'S OF ZION THE BEHAVIOR OF THIS ANTI-CHRIST SYSTEM DEMONSTRATING THE CHARACTERS LIKE DERANGE DEMONS DRAGONS SERPENT GRIZZLY BEARS ROARING, GROWLING FULL OF THEMSELVES WITH MISCHIEVOUS ANGER HOSTILITY TORMENTING SPIRITS.

WER'RE MOST DEFINITELY ENTERING INTO A NEW TIME OF ERA, WITH BIRTHING PAINS FOR EXAMPLE WHEN WOMAN GIVEN AND CONCIEVING CHILD. GOD'S ESTABLISHING A NEW WORLD ORDER SYSTEM THE OLD WALLS HAS FALLEN THERE'S MUST BECOME A RECREATION OF A KINGDOM SYSTEM MUST BE PUT INTO PLACE. GOD'S SIMPLY SAYING OR DEMONSTRATING EITHER YOUR'RE FOR ME OR YOU'RE AGAINST ME. IT'S TIME FOR THE SHOW DOWN HE'S SEPARATING THE WHEAT FROM THE TARES ESCAPING THE LION'S BEARS CLAWS THE REAPERS ARE THE ANGELS SENT TO REAP THE FIELD. THE TARES BOUND AND BURNED ARE THE EVIL ONES SEPARATED OUT AND CAST INTO FIRE PUNISHMENT AT THE JUDGMENT.THE WHEAT GATHERED

INTO THE BARN REPRESENT THE RIGHTEOUS WHO ARE SEPARATED OUT AND MADE TO SHINE FORTH IN THE KINGDOM OF THE FATHER.

"A SPOKEN WORD"
AMOS 5:19 AS IF A MAN DID FLEE FROM A LION AND A BEAR.

AMOS 3:4 WILL A LION ROAR IN THE FOREST, WHEN HE HATH NO PREY? WILL A YOUNG LION CRY OUT OF HIS DEN, IF HE HAVE TAKEN NOTHING?

THEE HANDS OF THE LORD WAS UPON THEM TO EXIT FROM EGYPT ITS ABOUT LEAVING A PLACE OR SITUATION.

MITZRAYIM IS THE HEBREW AND ARAMIC NAME FOR THE LAND OF EGYPT.

1 PETER 4:12 BELOVED, THINK IT NOT STRANGE COCERNING THE FIERY TRAIL WHICH IS TO TRY YOU, AS THOUGH SOME STRANGE THING HAPPENED UNTO YOU;

THE HOUR HAS COME MINISTERING ANGELS REVELATION.

DEAR CHILD OF GOD

BEHOLD ANOTHER MID-NIGHT VISITAION ON JANUARY 16, 2022 WHAT A DEEP REVELATION THERE'S A CLEAR SENSE OF A STRONG DOWNLOAD INSTRUCTIONS SPOKEN UNTO ME A URGENT WARNING ALERT SOUNDING THE TRUMPETS CLARION CALLS IN HIS HOUR COMING DESTRUCTIONS THE CITIES WE SHALL NOT BE MOVE ABOUT WHAT WE'VE HEARD NOR SEE. DAY OF GOD'S WRATH HOWEVER THIS SITUATION IS HAPPENING ALL AROUND US ON EVERY FOUR CORNERS HAS CREEP UPON THE DEEP FACE OF EARTH KEEP WATCH ASTRONOMIC CLIMATE DISASTERS FLOODS FIRE DISEASE RUMORS OF WARS WIDE SPREAD HUMANS MATERIAL ECONOMICS OR ENVIRONMENTAL CALAMIY AND LOSSES MOREOVER ELOHIM, ELSHADDAI HAS COME TO FOREWARN HIS PEOPLE OH! KEEP WATCH DAY OR NIGHT FOR THE HOURS OF UNEXPECTED END TIMES HAS ARRIVED. I'AM HAS SENT ME AS A PROACTIVE C I A FRONT-RUNNER GIVEN FORESIGHT TO PROVIDE IMPORTANT REVELATION WISDOM OR KNOWLEDGE BY STANDING IN THE GAP TO HELP LIFT AND STRENGTHEN THOSE WHO'S STILL ASLEEP IN THEIR CAVES OUR MASTER REDEEMER CALLING FORTH EACH ONE TO REMOVE MAN'S GRAVE

CLOTHES BY PUTTING ON THE FULL ARMOR ABLE TO WITH STAND GREAT FORCES OF DEPRESSION SUPPRESSION AND OPPRESSION.

THE FINAL WORDS FOR TODAY IS A PROPHETIC REVELATION MOCK GOD, HOLY SPIRIT, HIS CHILDREN AND GROUPS OF PEOPLE WAY FAR BEYOND ONE'S MEASURE. THE JOKE IS OVER IT'S TIME TO STEP UP AND GET IN ORDER.

"BABYLONIA EMPIRE HAS FALLEN"

THE ALARMS HAS BEGUN WE'RE LIVING IN A UNPRECEDENT TIME WITH SUCH CURRENT EVENTS THAT IS UNFOLDING THRU WORLD WIDE HISTORICAL END TIMES BIBLICAL PROPHECY COMING TO PASS.

BEHOLD I'LL DO A NEW THING SAYS THE LORD IT'S TIME FOR A NEW SEASON. AFTER ALL BATTLES AND GREAT CALAMITY GOD'S REMNANT OF PEOPLE REMAIN STANDING GREAT MIGHTY WARRIORS.

TOUCH THE HEM OF HIS GARMENT MIRCALES OF HEALING.

GOD'S MIGHTY HANDS PERFORMING WHAT A GLORIOUS EXPERIENCE IN WORLD TIME HISORICAL GREAT MOMENT ON THIS DAY JANUARY 22, 2022 WE'RE ON A 21 DAY'S FAST, AMONGST THE CONGREATION AS WELL; WITH MY SISTER IN CHRIST AND I SUGGESTIONS WERE TO COME TOGETHER IN PRAYER AND AGREEMENT ON THE BEHALF OF THIS INDIVIDUAL WHO HAPPENS TO BE MY PRAYER PARTNER GOOD FRIEND. THIS PERSON HAS BEING WAITING APPROXIMATELY 10 LONG YEARS FOR A LUNG TRANSPLANT. WE STOOD CAME TOGETHER IN AGREEMENT STANDING IN THE GAP REQUESTING PETITIONING, DECREEING AND DECLARING SPEAKING THOSE THINGS INTO EXISTENCING BEHOLD BREAKING NEWS GUEST WHAT? GOOD NEWS LOOK AT THE HAND OF OUR ABBA FATHER OUR REQUEST WAS GRANTED SHE OBTAINED FAVOR ALSO RECEIVED TWO LUNGS THE POWER OF GREATNESS MANIFESTING THERE'S SIGNS OF SUPERNATURAL, AMAZING REMARKABLE HEALING WONDERS HER HEALTH BEING RESTORED THIS PERSON WAS BURDEN DOWN WITH CARRING MANY OXYGEN TANKS EACH DAY WHAT AN EXCITING THRILLED, AWESOME MIRACLE NOW LET'S PAUSE FOR A MOMENT TO REFLECT WE'RE JUST IN THE FIRST MONTH OF JANUARY THIRD WEEK WHAT A DIVINE OMINIPOTENT, ALL

POWERFUL OMINISCIENT ALL KNOWING OMINPRESENT SUPREMELY GOOD IN OTHER WORD GOD KNOWING EVERYTHING.

ISAIAH 53:5 BUT HE WAS WOUNDED FOR OUR TRANSGRESSIONS, HE WAS BRUISED FOR OUR INQUITIES THE CHASTISEMENT FOR OUR PEACE WAS UPON HIM AND BY HIS STRIPES, WE ARE HEALED THE ULTIMATE PLAN OF GOD IS NOT DIVINE HEALING BUT DIVINE HEALTH.

ISAIAH 54:17 NO WEAPON THAT IS FORMED AGAINST THEE SHALL PROSPER: AND EVERY TONGUE THAT SHALL RISE AGAINST THEE IN JUDGMENT THOU SHALT CONDEMN.

WHAT THE DEVIL MEANT FOR EVIL?

GOD WILL USE FOR GOOD HE LOVES YOU AND WHAT SATAN MEANS FOR EVIL IN YOUR LIFE HE MEANS FOR GOOD KEEP YOUR EYE'S ON HIM.

GLORY TO GLORY! THERE'S LIFE, HEALING, HEALTH PROTECTION RESTORATION, TRANSFORMATION AND RESURRECTION WONDEROUS WORKING POWER IN THE BLOOD.

"THOU ART MERCIFUL"

MARK 5:34 MAY GOD GIVE YOU PEACE, YOU ARE HEALED, AND YOU WILL NO LONGER BE IN PAIN, AND HE SAID TO HER: DAUGHTER, THY FAITH HATH MADE THEE WHOLE GO IN PEACE. NEVERTHELESS, SIGNIFICANTLY THERE'S EVEN GREATER SUPERNATURAL POWER WHEN TRUSTING, WALKING BY FAITH TO TOUCH THE HEM OF HIS GARMENT.

"THE FAITHFUL SURVIVOR"

AS FOR YOU, YOU MEANT EVIL AGAINST ME, BUT GOD MEANT IT FOR GOOD, TO BRING IT ABOUT THAT MANY PEOPLE SHOULD BE KEPT ALIVE, AS THEY ARE TODAY.

"GOD'S POWER IN THE BLOOD STILL WORKS"

MATTHEW 18:19 AGAIN, TRULY I TELL YOU THAT IF TWO OF YOU ON EARTH AGREE ABOUT ANYTHING THEY ASK FOR, IT WILL BE DONE FOR THEM BY MY FATHER IN HEAVEN.

"O KING OF MAJESTY"

THE HOUR HAS COME A WOMEN IS CROWN BY DELIVERANCE, HEALING.

THANK YOU!
KING OF KING'S

MAN'S RAGING INTERNAL/ WARFARE WITIN HIS OWN MASS DESTRUCTION.

MAN'S INTERNAL WARFARE ON FEBRUARY 15, 2022 I WAS PROMPT TO SHARE, AND BRING FORTH THIS MESSAGE.

WHAT IS KARMA?

WHAT IS A WITCH?

KARAM IS ACTUALLY IDEALISTIC A CLASSY WISE REALITY THAT WILL CALMLY SIT YOU DOWN AND SERVE YOU A DELICIOUS CUP OF TEA YOU'LL EITHER SOON REALIZED IN ADDITION OR PERHAPS TYPICALLY IN ACTUALITY THE SAME SUBSTANCE TOXINS LACED WITH POISON YOU SERVED OTHER'S FOR MANY YEAR'S, WATCH OUT BE EXTREMELY CAUTIOUS STAY ALERT WHAT WAS INTENED FOR OTHER'S NOW HAS OVERTURN SO THERFORE WITCHES WHO SET THOSE TRAPS MUST FALL TASTE THEIR HIGHLY PLEASANT TOXIN POISON THEMSELVES.

MAN'S INTERNAL CONFLICT EMOTIONAL DISODERLY BEHAVIOR VS MAN'S LACK OF TRUE IDENTITY, AND INTERGRITY OF WHO AM I.

BE EXTREMELY VERY CAUTIOUS HOW YOU SERVE YOUR TEA. BECAUSE YOUR OWN MASS WEAPONS OF DESTRUCTION WILL DESTROY YOUR INNER SOUL MAN.

WE'VE COME TO THIS CONCULSION IT'S CALLED THE BATTLE OF MAN'S MIND, WALKING IN THE SPIRIT. DEFEATING OVERCOMING THE FLESH FURTHERMORE, ACCELERATING TOWARDS LOVE, PEACE FREEDOM, AND JUSTICE HAVING THE POWER TO OVERTHROW EVIL-DARKNESS TO EXPERIENCE A MORAL VICTORY.

DO NOT NEGLECT TO SHOW HOSPITALITY TO STRANGERS, FOR BY SO DOING GOD KNOWS THE HEART OF MAN.

"GOD JUDGES MAN'S HEART"

HEBREWS 13:2 BE NOT FORGETFUL TO ENTERAIN STRANGERS: FOR THERE BY SOME HAVE ENTERAINED ANGELS UNWARES.

1 SAMUEL 16:7 YOU BELIEVE YOU HAVE A SINCERE HEART. YOU BELIEVE, THEREFORE. THAT GOD ACCEPTS YOU. THE BIBLE AGREES THAT GOD KNOWS YOUR HEARTS. GOD SAID TO SAMUEL THAT HE SEES NOT AS MAN SEES: "MAN LOOK ON THE OUTWARD APPEARANCE, BUT THE LORD LOOKS ON THE HEART"

"LISTEN TO A PARABLE"

PSALM 37:32 THE WICKED WATCHETH THE RIGHTEOUS, AND SEEKETH TO SLAY HIM WICKED MEN HATE RIGHTEOUS MEN:

CRACKING COLD CASE MURDER MYSTERIES Pt. 2

BEHOLD UNFOLDING AND DECODING A COLD CASE MURDER MYSTERIES. ON THIS DAY FEBRUARY 07, 2022 WOW AND WOW! THE SIGNS OF WONDER'S, GLORY HALLELUJAH THE HEAVENS PORTERS HAS OPEN THIS IS A REVIVAL MOMENT IN HISTORCIAL TIME ERA OUR ABBA FATHER AND I ARE CONNECTING IN SUCH A GREAT MIGHTY MOVE PROPHETIC POWERFUL WAY FROM THE THRONE OF GLORY TO EARTH REALM. LET'S PAUSE FOR A MOMENT HERE MY SON AND I STEPS ARE TRULY DEFINITELY IN ALIGNMENT WITH THE WILL OF GOD NOT TO MENTION WE'VE BEING SUMMONS FOR A GREAT COMMISSION SUCH A TIME AS THIS. THE IMPORTANTS OF THE MATTER IS MY SON AND I WAS LED BY THE SPIRIT TO PARTNER UP WITH GOD, HIS HOLY ANGEL'S AND OF COURSE THE NEVIGATION SYSTEM WHICH REFERS BY HOLY GHOST WE CAME INTO SUBMISSION IN ODER TO HELP CRACKING THIS COLD CASE MURDER MYSTERY INTO THIS PART OF REGION HOWEVER PETITIONING PRAYER'S SUPPLICATION REQUEST DECREES, DECLARATION AND EXECUTIONS WAS WELL INFORMED TO PUT INTO EFFECT BY EVER PRECAUTIONARY THE SOLUTION AS A RESULT REQUESTING ON THE BEHALF OF FALLEN VICTIMS THAT WE FIND FAVOR IN THE SIGHT OF GOD AND ALL MAN IN ADDITION ANTICIPATING TO DRIVE OUT ALL EVIL DARKNESS, NEGATIVE FORCES, BY LAW'S OF

ACTION, MOREOVER RESOLVING A HEART OF MATTERS BUT OF COURSE WE'RE WALKING BY FAITH TAKEN BOLD STEP'S WAS A BIG RISK TAKER. THE TWO SUSPECTS ARE NOW APPREHENDED CHARGE WITH 31 COUNTS JUST TO NAME A FEW MURDER, HOMICIDS AND A HOST OF OTHER ILLEGAL ACTIVITIES IT'S A HONOR AND PRIVILEGE BY OBTAINING, HAVING ACCESS WITH DEMONSTRATING ASTONISHING THE INVISIBLE TANGIBLE SUERNATURAL POWERFUL TOUCH BY THE SOVEREIGNTY SUPREME GOD SPECIAL METHOD SYSTEM THESE ARE GOD'S SPECIAL SECRETS DECODING COLD CASE MURDER CRIMES MYSTERY. BREAKING NEWS REPORT FOUR MONTHS LATER MY DIVINE POWERFUL PROPHETIC PROPHECY AND PREDICTION CAME TO PASS ON 02/07/2022.

GOD'S SECRET INTELLIGENT AGENTS CONVERTING SECRET CODES, MESSAGES BY ANALYZING OR INTERPRETING CONDUCTING ESPIONAGE CONNECTIONS, ACTIVITIES INSIDE BEHIND MANY SENSES SERVING THE KINGDOM REALM SPIRITUAL WORLD.

"WALKING IN THE FIELDS OF DRY BONE'S"

JOB 22:28 THOU SHALT ALSO DECREE A THING, AND IT SHALL BE ESTABLISHEED UNTO THEE: AND THE LIGHT SHALL SHINE UPON THY WAYS.

"A FAITHFUL SERVANT"

WE'RE ALL GRANTED ACCESS BUT ARE YOU WILLING TO PUT DOWN THE WEAPONS PICKUP YOUR BIBLE AND CARRY THE CROSS?

"A TIME OF TROUBLE"

GOLIATH THOUGHT THAT DAVID WAS A SMALL LITTLE BOY WITH NO SENSE OF POWER NO FIGHT. HE THOUGHT HE WAS JUST A NO BODY A NOTHING! HE SOON FOUND OUT DIFFERENTLY, THEM SAME PEOPLE THAT EVERY, BODY CALLED A NOBODY IS THE VERY SAME PEOPLE THAT GOD COULD BE USING TO CHANGE THE WORLD. MAKE NO MISTAKE GOD DOES'NT NEED ANYBODY PERMISSION TO USE YOU YOU'RE SIMPLY CALLED AND CHOSEN. BEFORE THE FOUNDATION OF THE WORLD.

EVERYTHING THAT THE ENEMY WAS USING AGAINST ME IS WORKING IN MY FAVOR RIGHT NOW! THE ENEMY THOUGHT HE WAS GOING TO DESTROY ME AND TAKE ME OUT. BUT GOD USED IT TO BUILD MY SPIRITUAL MUSCLES GOD USED IT TO BUILD ME UP FOR ALL BATTLES BUT WHAT THE ENEMY MEANT FOR BAD GOD USED IT FOR MY GOOD. IT'S HELPING TO BUILD YOU UP FOR SPIRITUAL WARFARE IT'S MAKING ME STRONGER AND STRONGER SO THERFORE IF CHRIST KEEPING GIVING ME HIS POWER. I WILL GLADLY BRAG ABOUT HOW WEAK I'AM YES! I'AM GLAD TO BE WEAK, BECAUSE WHEN I'AM WEAK I'AM STRONG GOD KEEPS MAKING ME STRONGER AND STRONGER HALLELUJAH.

DEAR CHILD OF GOD COME GO WITH ME ON THIS EXCITING ADVENTUROUS JOURENY BY EXPLORING INTO THE KINGDOM WORLD OF MYSTERY SPEAK YOUR VISIONS INTO REALITY STAY FOCUS AND MASTER YOUR MIND, HEART, DREAMS AND VISION'S NEXT STEP YOU SHALL ARRIVE ACCORDING TO MAN'S DESIRES.

MANY WILL MARVEL BUT SOME WILL BE JEALOUS WHY?

THE ENEMY IS FIGHTING YOU FIERCELY BE STRONG AND COURAGEOUS GOD IS WITH YOU.

WHAT DOES IT MEAN TO BE A SON OR DAUGHTER OF GOD? I'AM YOU ARE THE OFFSPRING OF DEITY WE'RE LITERAL DESCENDANT'S OF A DIVINE FATHER INHERITING GODLY ATTRIBUTES AND POTENTIAL.

WHAT IS THE GREATEST SIN IN THE BIBLE? BLASPHEMY AGAINST THE HOLY SPIRIT ALSO KNOW AT THE SIN UNTO DEATH.
ARE YOU BLASPHEMING OR MOCKING GOD HOLY SPIRIT AND MANKIND?
ARE YOU A BUSY BODY?
ARE YOU A VISIONARY?
ARE YOU A TRAIL BLAZER?
ARE YOU CARRYING THE MANTEL?

MARK 3:29 BUT HE THAT SHALL BLASPHEME AGAINST THE HOLY GHOST HATH NEVER FORGIVENESS, BUT IS IN DANGER OF ETERNAL DAMNATION:

CONVERSATIONS SPOKEN CONNECTING TELECOMMUNICATIONS TRANSMITTER HIGH FREQUENCY UNIVERSAL ENERGY ALL POWER'S

ON THIS PARTICULAR DAY FEBRUARY 04, 2022 I BEGIN THE MORNING ROUTINE BY PREPARING MY TWO GRAND DAUGHTER'S FOR SCHOOL MOREOVER I HAD MENTION TO THE THREE YEAR OLD ABOUT NOT ABLE TO SEE MY GRANDSON, SHE THEN REPLY BY ASKING ME GRANDMA, IS YOUR GRANDSON YOUR SON IMMEDIATELY MY RESPONSE WAS NO HE'S MY GRANDCHILD LIKE YOU'RE BUT ANY HOW LATER ON THAT EVENING MY GREATER INTUITION SPIRIT MAN LEAP. LET'S PAUSE FOR BRIEF MOMENT I LOOKED OVER AT THE CLOCK IT WAS ALMOST 6:30pm NEVERTHELESS, I PROCEED PERPARING DINNER FOR THE

GIRL'S. WHILE STANDING INSIDE THE KITCHEN MY NEXT THOUGHTS WERE CONSIDERING OR CONTEMPLATING RATHER TO CALL HIM TO NIGHT OR TOMORROW FURTHERMORE BESIDES FROM THAT MY NEXT THOUGHTS WAS HIS MOTHER NEVER EVEN CALLS ME. SO THAT BEING SAID A FEW HOURS LATER PASSES BY AT THIS VERY POINT I DECIDED TO EAT DINNER NOW ON THIS PARTICULAR NIGHT BETWEEN 9:00pm OR PERHAPS 9:30pm. BREAKING NEWS ALERT BEHOLD SUDDENLY APPROXIMATELY NO EVEN A FEW SECONDS THE TELEPHONE RINGS ON THE OTHER END MY GRAND SON MOTHER CALLS AND SAY'S YOUR GRANDBABY WANTS TO SPEAK WITH YOU WE THEN BRIEFLY CONVERSATED AMONGST EACH OTHER MY REACTIONS WAS GREAT TEARS OF JOY WHAT A PHENOMENAL SUPER DIVINE INTERVENTION, THE AIR WAVES PICKUP THE FREQUENCY FROM THE ELECTRICAL SHOCK OF MY HEART'S DESIRES. SUCH A MARVELOUS MIRACULOUS SIGNS AND WONDERS OH YEAH! HE'S A WONDER DEEP IN MY SOUL. BASED UPON MY FATHER LOVE GRACE AND MERCY WOW! AMAZING REMARKABLE SOVEREIGNTY SUPREME BEING TRANSCENDING SPIRTIUAL POWERS MANIFESTING DIRECTLY THROUGH GOD'S TECHNOLOGY DEVICES.

WHAT A MIGHTY ACT OF GOD'S HANDS
WHAT A DIVINE HOOKUP
WHAT A SURPRISE

THE HUMAN'S HEART

1 CORINTHIANS 2:2-4-11 AND I, BRETHREN WHEN I CAME TO YOU, CAME NOT WITH EXCELLENCY OF SPEECH OR OF WISDOM DECLARING UNTO YOU THE TESTIMONY OF GOD.

2:4 AND MY SPEECH AND MY PREACHING WAS NOT WITH ENTICING WORDS OF MAN'S WISDOM, BUT IN DEMONSTRATION OF THE SPIRITS AND OF POWER:

2:11 WHO CAN SEE INTO A MAN'S HEART AND KNOW HIS THOUGHTS? ONLY THE SPIRIT THAT DWELLS WITHIN THE MAN. IN THE SAME WAY. THE THOUGHTS OF GOD ARE KNOW ONLY BY HIS SPIRIT.

CRACKING COLD CASE SPIRITUAL WARFARE MYSTRIES Pt. 2

THE MYSTRIES BEHIND SPIRITUAL WARFARE ATTACKS FROM A SUPERNATURAL POINT OF VIEW LET'S REWIND THE FILM I'VE MENTION PRIOR TO PREVIOUS MONTHS AGO WAY BACK ON OCTOBER 24, 2021 I RECEIVED A DREAM PERTAINING LIONS, TIGERS AND WOLVES WHILE IN THIS VISION THOSE FOUR FOOT LEGGED BEAST STOOD ALL AROUND ME, THEY KEPT ATTEMPTING TO TEASE, TANTE TORMENTING AND CHARGING AGAINST ME. LET'S PAUSE FOR A BRIEF MOMENT IN THE NIGHT VISITATION WAS A DIRECT, INDICATION OF REVELATION TO FOREWARN ME ABOUT THE SIGNS STAY ALERT AND CAUTION FOR DANGER PENDING UP AHEAD ON THIS PATH CALLED OUR GREATEST ALLIES WATCH OUT SNEAKY SECRET ATTACKS.

MOREOVER LET'S FAST FORWARD THIS FILM STAY CAUTION THERE'S EVIL DARK FORCES LURKING INTO THE SECOND HEAVENS IT'S CALL DEMONIC REALM. BEHOLD THIS UNTHINKABLE RANDOM ACT OCCURRED ON THIS PARTICULAR DAY MARCH 07, 2022 I'VE RECEIVED A PHONE CALL FROM THIS PERSON ACTING EXTREMELY OBNOXIOUS VERY OFFENSIVE WITH HATRED TOWARDS ME FOR NO CAUSE OR GOOD REASON BESIDES THIS INDIVIDUAL BEHAVIOR WAS ANNOYING AGGRESTIVE NEVERTHELESS,

DEAR CHILD OF GOD HOLD ON STAND STRONG BE BOLD COURAGEOUS BECAUSE THESE DARK LOW ENERGY ENTITY RISING UP STARTING TO BEGIN THROWING SHADE AN THEIR EVIL DEVICES WEAPONS SUCH AS DISCORD DIVISION, AFFLICTION STRIFE, TENSION TORMENTING TRYING TO CAUSE SOMEONE TO FEEL DEEPLY HURT, UPSET OR ANGRY TOWARDS MANKIND SOUL. IT'S CRAZY BIZARRE THEY'RE NOT QUITE AWARE THAT I CAN PICKUP MAN'S ENERGY LIKE A RADAR OR EVEN DISCREN GOOD AND EVIL HOWEVER THIS NEGATIVE LOW IQ VIBERATIONAL PERSON MAIN MOTIVES, OBJECTIVE TO DISCREDT, DECEIVING DISPISING MOCKING BLASPHEMING SETTING TRAPS TO DESTROY OTHER'S FURTHEMORE WHEN PEOPLE WITH UNPLEASANT HEART'S SPEAK UNKINDNESS RUDENESS WORDS OR EVEN NASTY COMMENTS ABOUT YOU. ALL WAYS REMEMBER ONE THING OTHER PEOPLE ARE IRRELEVANT THEIR OPINIONS IT'S NOT IMPORTANT SECONDLY IT DOES'NT EVEN MATTER. WE MUST ALSO DISCREN OR RECOGNIZE THEIR CHARATERISTIC ATTRIBUTES THIS CERTAIN GROWLING UNRESTED SPIRITS COME TO KILL STEAL, DESTROY THE CHILDERN OF THE LIGHT. KEEP A WATCH OUT THEY'RE DISPLAYING, REFLECTION OF WHO THEY'RE REPRESENTING FROM A LOW DARK KINGDOM WORLD HELLO! AMERICA STAY TUNE ALER WATCH OUT THESE ARE SATANIC WITCHES THE HELPER OF THE FATHER OF MANY LIES AND CONFUSION. YAHWEH THE GREATEST I'AM GIVEN HIS PEOPLE WARFARE BATTLES INSTRUCTIONS AND PREPARATION TO DIRECT MAN'S TASK OR MISSION BY ALL MEANS NECESSARY NEVER ALLOW ANYONE WHO HAPPENS TO BE RUDE OR MAYBE INCONSIDERATE TO DOWNPLAY OVER POWER YOU BY LEAVING ONESELF VULNERABLE TO THE DEGREE YOU BECOME IRRITATED, SPEECHLESS, SENSLESS CONFUSED AND POWERLESS I REPEAT NEVER ALLOW PEOPLE TO STEAL YOUR GOD GIVEN

SUPERPOWER'S AND PEACE, JOY ALWAYS OVERCOME EVIL WITH GOOD.

DISCONNECTION DISCORD DISEMPOWERMENT FROM THE MOST HIGH GOD OF THIS UNIVERSE USUALLY STEM FROM A LACK OF SPIRITUAL UNDERSTANDING AND AWARENESS WHICH CAUSES MAN'S STATE OF MINDS, HEARTS STARTS SUFFERING, FAILING DUE TO DIS-EASED CAUSED BY STRESS IN ADDITIONALLY WHEN MAN FUNCTIONING BY OPERATING IN HIS OWN AUTHORITY AND DEFAULTS FOR A LACK OF LOVE AND HARMONY WE'RE DEFINITELY LIVING IN A TIME OF ERA MAN IS ATTACKING OTHERS BY INTIMIDATING OR BULLYING IN SUCH AWAY THEY'RE PROJECTING THEIR OWN INSECURITY UPON YOU.

RESIST TEMPTATION FROM LUCIFER AND HIS FALLEN AGENTS THEY WILL FLEE; JUST CALL UPON JESUS CHRIST AND DECLARE THE BLOOD WATCH THEM DISAPPEARED, BE STILL AND LET GOD FIGHT YOUR BATTLES.

"THE ENEMIES WILL NEVER OUT SMART GOD"

I'AM CALLED, COMMISSION TO BE A GLOBAL WARRIOR, CHANGE AGENT BY HELPING A WOUNDED SOLDIER WHO'S FALLEN DOWN BY THE WAYSIDE IN MAN'S OWN RUINS GOD WILL EXPOSED EVERY STUMBLING BLOCK, TRAP SET BY THE ENEMY.

"PHYSICAL EMOTIONAL ATTACKS"

MAN'S FIGHTING HIS INNER DEMONS CALLED INNER MAN'S CONFLICTS OF WAR WITH HIS OWN MASS DESTRUCTION OUR FINAL CONCLUSION MAN WILL EITHER RISE FROM THE DEFEAT OF ASHES TO LIVE EVER LASTING ETERNAL OR

HE WILL SET IN HIS OWN PIT OF SIN HELL AND TORMENT EVER LASTING JUDGEMENT.

"THOU ART MERCIFUL"

JOHN 10:10 "THE THIEF COMES ONLY TO STTEAL AND KILL AND DESTROY; I CAME THAT THEY MAY HAVE LIFE AND HAVE IT IN ABUNDANCE"

WATCH OUT SIEGE FIRE AMBUSH ATTACK'S Pt. 2

WATCH OUT CRACKING COLD CASE MYSTREY FROM THE SUPERNATURAL REALM. BACK ON OCTOBER 24, 2021 I RECEIVED A PROPHETIC NIGHT VISITATION PERTAINING THESE FOUR FOOT LEGGED BEAST WHICH WERE WOLVES, LIONS, TIGERS THAT STOOD ALL AROUND ME. THEY KEPT ATTEMPTING TO CHARGE TANTING TEASEING AND TORMENTING AGAINST MY POOR LITTLE SOUL LET'S PAUSE FOR A SECOND MOREOVER THE HOLY ANGELS WAS A DIRECT INDICATION WITH DEEP REVELATION TO FORTELL INFORM ME WATCH OUT STAY ALERT FOR DANGER SIGNS UP AHEAD THE ROAD CALLED OUR GREATEST ALLIES ATTACKS IN ADDITION THIS PARTICULAR REVELATION WAS GIVEN SO THEREFORE I CAN GRID UP MY LOINS GET READY FOR HARD WORK OR BATTLES IN ACTUALITY THE LORD WAS PREPARING AND STRENGTHEN ME FOR WHAT IS TO COME. LET'S MOVE ALONG NOW FURTHERMORE ON THIS DAY MARCH 20, 2022 6 MONTHS LATER I RECEIVE A SUDDEN KNOCK ON THE DOOR I THEN PROCEED TO LOOK OUT THE PEEP HOLE, SECONDLY I THEN OPEN THIS PERSON SO HAPPEN TO BE A FAMILY MEMBER NEVERTHELESS SHE BEGAIN TO EXPLAIN ABOUT A SITUATION THAT PERHAPS WENT DOWN, THEN NEXT I PROCEEDED TO ASK A QUESTION WHY THAT CERTAIN THING HAPPEN TO HER OH BOY! WHY DID I JUST ASK FOR ONE SIMPLE QUESTION.

I MEAN THIS ANGRY GROWLING TONY THE TIGER AROUSING WITH SO MUCH BITTER ANGUISH BUILD UP INSIDE THE INTERNAL MAN SHE WENT OFF BY STARTING ATTACKING ME WITH SUCH VICIOUS CRUEL WORD'S SUCH AS YOUR STUPID I'AM CRAZY, HOMELESS SHE KEPT ON TRYING TO INSULT PUTTING ME DOWN TALKING ABOUT MY BOOKS PLUS NOT ONLY THAT SHE HAD THE NERVOUS TO MENTION HOW I SPEND OR INVEST MY MONEY THAT WHICH HOWEVER I WORK HARD FOR SO IN OTHER WORDS SHE TRYING TO DICTATE MY LIFE THEY'RE MAD BECAUSE I'AM PURSUING MY GOD GIVEN DREAM'S AND STEPPING INTO DESTINY WOW! NEEDLESS TO SAY THIS HOSTILE AGGRESTIVE LOW IQ VIBERATION INDIVIDUAL IS LACKING, LOVE, COMPASSIONATE TOWARDS ALL MANKIND PEOPLE ACTUALLY BLASPHEMING, AND DISREPECTING OTHER'S THEY'RE LITERALLY WALKING TO AND FRO SEEKING WHOM THEY CAN PROJECT THEIR INSECURITY UPON AND PROVOKE TO ANGER. THESE TYPE OF SPIRITS I CAN DISCERN GOOD VS EVIL THEY'RE NOT FOOLING ME WHAT SOEVER. LET'S PAUSE ONCE AGAIN FOR A BRIEF MOMENT BACK ON FEBRUARY 17, 2022 NOW PLEASE STAY WITH ME HERE I'AM ABOUT TO UNFOLD ANOTHER NIGHT VISITATION THAT WAS DOWNLOADED INTO MY SPIRITMAN BEHOLD I HAD A VISION THIS HUGE ASTRONOMICAL HUMONGOUS BLACK ANACONDA SNAKE. THIS CREATURE WAS LYING STRETCH EXPANSE ACROSS THE LAND. VERY CREEPY I MUST SAY. LET'S MOVE FORWARD REMIND YOU WER'RE GOING DEEPER UP THE ROAD HERE STAY WITH ME. THIS INDIVIDUAL I'AM REFERRING TO SHE HAS ALWAYS HAD A STRONG DEEP COMPASSION, FEELING DESIRES TO WORSHIP THESE TYPE OF REPTILES, SHE EVEN CALLS HERSELF MS. ANACONDA ARE YOU STILL WITH ME HERE? OKAY LET'S CONTINUE ON NOW I'VE BEING DEALING WITH THIS PERSON BEHAVIOR FOR NEARLY 51 YRS, I'M NOT TO TRASH OR BASH ANYONE

I MUST HOWEVER COME TO FORETELL OR FOREWARN PEOPLE LIKE SUCH I'LL WILL INTENTIONS TOWARDS ALL MANKIND. BESIDES FROM THAT SHE HAS ALWAYS HAD A DEEP SENSE OF ANXIETY OR LACK OF SELFCONFIDNCE AND INSECURITY NONETHELESS PEOPLE ARE NAVIGATING THROUGH THE DEPTHS OF THE EARTH WITH A SENSE OF SPECIAL TREATMENT, ENTITLEMENT WHEN INFACT THEY MENTION THE LOVE FOR GOD, JESUS CHRIST. BUT YOU DISPLAY HATRED TOWARDS YOUR OWN BLOOD BROTHER'S OR SISTER'S AND NEIGHBORED. JUST KNOW WHEN WER'RE DISPLAYING THIS CERTAIN BEHAVIOR CHARACTERISTIC TRAITS YOU'RE SIMPLY MOCKING, OR BLASTPHEMING DISHONORING GOD AND THE HOLY SPIRIT GRIEVE NOT THE SPIRIT GET RID OF ALL BITTERNESS RAGE ANGER HARSH WORD AND SLANDER AS WELL.

"WALKING BY FAITH IN THE PATH OF DISCRENMENT"

WALKING IN THE FIELDS OF THE UNKNOWN WATCH OUT SIEGE FIRE AMBUSHED ATTACKS ONCE AGAIN UNEXPLANABLE STRANGE MYSTERIOUS DEMONIC ACTIVITIES FAR BEYOND MAN'S NATURE EYE'S ONLY TO UNDERSTAND OR COMPREHENED FROM THE SUPERNATURAL DIVINE POWER'S BECAREFUL AND MINDFUL OF INCONSIDERATED PEOPLE THERE'S A MYSTERY BEYOND AND BEHIND MAN'S MOTIVES, ACTIONS A TAUNTING TORMENTING PUSH UP BULLY STUBBORN REBELLOUS SPIRITS LET'S MOVE ALONG NOW OH YEAH! I'M READY TO DIVE IN THIS STORY FOR A FEW MINUTES I FORGOT TO MENTION THE UNFAVORABLE OUT COME OF THIS PERSON WAS UNSUCCESSFUL NOT CERTAIN TO WIN OR SUCCEED. RESIST THE EVIL ONE'S AND THEIR TEMPTATIONS THEY WILL FLEE HOW DARE THEM THINK THEY CAN CHALLENGE OR WIN ME I'AM WALKING WITH

GREAT MIGHTY SUPERPOWER'S WHO WILL'NT BE FORCE TO RECKON WITH.

"DAY'S OF TEMPTATION"

"WALKING WITH THE PRESENCES OF GOD"

WHEN GOD HIMSELF SPEAKS OR COMMANDS WHO WILL DARE TO DO OTHER WISE THAN OBEY?

GOD'S MIGHTY GENERALS UNDER ATTACK WATCH OUT FOR THE HIDDEN DANGEROUS SIGNS AHEAD. I'M HIGHLY ANOINTED A POWERFUL MIGHTY UNDERDOG WHO REFUSE TO BE PROVOKED BY SOME OUTRAGEOUSLY JEALOUS OR ENVY MISARABLE PERSON THAT THEY HAVE NO REASON BEHIND IT BOY OH BOY! THE DEVIL ADVOCATES IS TRULY UPSET WITH THEIR SELVES THEY'RE NOT WALKING, SURRENDING UNDER GOD'S TRUE DIVINE AUTHORITY IT'S TIME TO BOW DOWN AND SUBMIT AND REPEANT. NEVER UNDER ESTIMATE THE UNDERDOG ESPECIALLY THE PERSON WHO PEOPLE ASSUME IS LEAST LIKELY TO SUCCEED BASED ON THEIR SOCIAL STATUS, LACK OF EXPERIENCES KNOWLEDGE OR EVEN PERHAPS HOW THEY MEASURE UP TO OTHER'S WHO'S WINNING.

IT'S PRETTY IMPRESSIVE, EXTREMELY FASCINATING AND HILARIOUS I GET TO EXPERIENCE FIRSTHAND WATCHING THE ATTACKS UNFOLD IN THE FORENSIC DARK ROOM. BASCIALLY THIS PROCESS IS LIKE A FILM DEVELOPING IT'S ABSOLUTELY AMAZING. AWESOME, AND REMARKABLE FEELING TO HAVE SUCH PRIVILEGE OR OPPORTUNITY BY WATCHING THE GREAT ATTACKS WOW AN WOW! OUR FATHER HAS GIVEN ONE OF HIS DAUGHTER'S THE KEYS TO ACCESS HIS SECRET VAULT. IT'S TOTALLY A THRILLED

SITTING DOWN EATING A BOX OF CHOCOLATE AND POP-CORN WATCHING THIS FILM DEVELOP SUCH A BLAST WATCHING A PREVIEW SCENE OF ATTRACTION. YOU MEAN WE CAN HAVE ACCESS TO THE KINGDOM THRONE ONCE AGAIN FEAR TACTIC THAT CONTINUALLY RAISE IT'S UGLY HEAD. WHEN YOU'RE IN A SPIRITUAL WARFARE BATTLE ALWAYS REMEMBER ONE THING TO STAY HUMBLE AND CALM CONTINUE REMAIN STEADFAST UNMOVABLE, UNSTOPPABLE WE WRESTLE NOT WITH FLESH AND BLOOD WE'RE RAGGING WAR WITH THESE STUBBORN REBELLOUS ENTITY DARK FORCES.

"BE STILL FEAR NOT FOR I'AM WITH YOU"

DEAR CHILD OF GOD

STAND FIRM IN THIS CRITICAL HOUR YOU HAD TO GO THROUGH IN ORDER FOR GOD TO USE YOU HE HAD TO SECRETLY REVEAL HIMSELF THROUGH YOU. BY DEMONSTRATING EXPOSING DISCLOSURE OF MAN'S EVIL INTENTIONS PLOTS OR PLANS THE PREDICTION PROPHECIES OF TIME LINE WORLD CURRENT EVENT'S ARE BEING FULFILLED MANIFESTING IN TIME HISTORICAL UNPRECEDENTED ERA.

"WALKING IN THE FIELD'S OF GLORY"

AMOS 3:7 SURELY THE LORD WILL DO NOTHING, BUT HE REVEALETH HIS SECRET UNTO HIS SERVANTS THE PROPHETS.

LUKE 1:45 AND BLESSED IS SHE THAT BELIEVED: FOR THERE SHALL BE A PEFORMANCE OF THOSE THINGS WHICH WERE TOLD HER FROM THE LORD.

LUKE 1:71 THAT WE SHOULD BE SAVE FROM OUR ENEMIES, AND FROM THE HAND OF ALL THAT HATE US

"A TIME OF ADVERSITY AND TROUBLES"

WE'RE DEFINITELY IN AN UNPARALLELED EVOLVING SITUATION DEALING WITH MAN'S MIND AND HEART'S NOT TO MENTION MENTALLY UNSTABLE, ABNORMAL FREAKISH WEIRD UTTERLY DISTURBANCE UNRESTED DISORDER CONDUCT JUST ROAMING AIMLESSLY.

TIME SEASON'S VS TIME ZONE'S

STAY IN TUNE
STAY WATCHFUL
STAY FAITHFUL
STAY BOLD
STAY LOYAL
STAY OBEDIENT
STAY AT PEACE
STAY THE COURSE

STAY IN THE KNOWN
STAY IN PRAYER
STAY CALM
STAY INCOURAGE
STAY STAND WITH INTEGRITY
STAY IN HIS PRESENCE'S
STAY HUMBLE
STAY WITH LOVE, PATIENCE

STAY IN THE MASTER PLANS ADVENTURALLY HE WILL TEACH INFORM YOU BY GIVEN YOU THE KEYS TO ACCESS THE MOST GREATEST HIGHEST DEGREE WHICH MAN CAN ATTAIN, ACHIEVE TO SIT INSIDE A PROPHETIC MYSTERY MASTER CLASS IT'S CALLED DISCIPLINING MAN'S FLESH MINDING MASTER'S PROGRAM.

"MASTER'S ARE WORLD LEADER'S WHO SEE'S GOD'S PROVISION, PURPOSE AND PLANS"

"IF YOUR HEART IS BROKEN"

THE THIEVES WITHIN OR OUTSIDE OF YOUR TEMPLE OCCUPYING, INVADING EFFECTING MAN'S MINDS, HEART'S BY ROBBING THEIR INNER PEACE AND JOY.

UNLOCKING GOD'S SECRET MYSTERIES THE HIDDEN POWER'S WITHIN MAN CONSCIOUSNESS STATE OF BEING WE BECOME OUR OWN GREATER ALLIES WHEN A PERSON BRINGS DIVISION HE ALSO RELEASES CONFUSION WITHIN HIS OWN TEMPLE OR INSIDE THE CAMP OF OTHERS. I'VE COME TO THE CONCLUSION BY STUDYING, EXPERIENCING, DISCIPLINE CONDITIONING MY MIND FOR FORTY PLUS YEARS ON HOW I DISCOVERED MY TRUTH AUTHENTIC SENSE OF SELF AWARENESS FOR MY LIFE PURPOSE AND HOW YOU CAN ALSO DISCOVER YOUR SUPERPOWER'S ONLY IF YOU CAN IMAGINE THE POWER AND VALUE WE POSSESS WITHIN THE MIND, HEART AND THE TEMPLE OF MAN'S BODY ALWAYS REMEMBER ONE THING MY FATHER AND I BECOME ONE'NESS SECONDLY THE LORD HAS SOUGHT FOR HIMSELF A MAN AFTER HIS OWN HEART

1 SAMUEL 13:14 I HAVE FOUND DAVID THE SON OF JESSE, A MAN AFTER MY OWN HEART, WHO WILL DO ALL MY WILL.

"WELL INFORMED JUST ACTIVATE THE LAW'S OF ACTION"

HOLD ON DEAR CHILD OF GOD WHILE BEING FASELY ACCUSED OR PERSECUTED FOR MY NAME SAKE

"A SPOKEN WORD"

MARK 13:13 AND YE, SHALL BE, HATED OF ALL MEN FOR MY NAME SAKE: BUT HE THAT SHALL, ENDURE UNTO THE END, THE SAME SHALL BE SAVED.

UNDERSTANDING OR DISCOVERING, SECRETS OF THE MESSIANIC BIBLICAL PROPHECIES. UNLOCKING HIDDEN CODES FROM THE ANCIENT SCROLLS OF HEBREWS SCRIPTURES.

ROMANS 12:14 BLESS THEM WHICH PERSECUTE YOU: BLESS, AND CURSE NOT.

JOEL 3:10 LET THE WEAK SAY, I'AM STRONG.

ISAIAH 40:29 HE GIVE POWER TO THE WEAK. AND TO THOSE WHO HAVE NO MIGHT HE INCREASES STRENGTH.

GENESIS 50:20 BUT AS FOR YOU, YE THOUGHT EVIL AGAINST ME; BUT GOD MEANT IT UNTO GOOD,TO BRING TO PASS, AS IT IS THIS DAY, TO SAVE MUCH PEOPLE ALIVE.

"HELP MINE UNBELIEF"

ROMANS 13:1-2- LET EVERY SOUL BE SUBJECT UNTO THE HIGHER POWERS FOR THERE IS NO POWER BUT OF GOD:

THE POWERS THAT BEARE ORDINED OF GOD.

13:2 WHOSOEVER THEREFORE RESISTETH THE POWER, RESISTETH THE ORDINANCE OF GOD: AND THEY THAT RESIST SHALL RECEIVE TO THEMSELVES DAMNATION.

ROMANS 12:12 REJOICING IN HOPE, PATIENT IN TRIBULATION; CONTINUING INSTANT IN PRAYER.

1 PETER 5:7-8 CASTING ALL YOUR CARE UPON HIM. FOR HE CARETH FOR YOU.

5:8 BE SOBER, BE VIGILANT BECAUSE YOUR ADVESARY THE DEVIL, AS A ROARING LION, WALKETH ABOUT, SEEKING WHOM HE MAY DEVOUR:

"ELIJAH NAME IN HEBREW MEANS MY GOD IS YAHWEH"

ELIJAH IS ONE OF THE GREATEST PROPHETS OF ALL TIMES AND WHY HE WAS REJECTED BY THE PEOPLE OF HIS OWN DAY. GOD ALLOWS UNEXPLAINABLE EVENTS TO HAPPEN TO US TO HELP DEVELOP US SOTHEREFORE WE CAN BE MORE LIKE THE PROPHET ELIJAH.

"DESTRUCTION BEFORE HAND"

DESTRUCTION OF JERUSALEM FORETOLD SINCE THE LORD IS SPEAKING TO THE JEWS, THIS MEANS THAT IF GOD HAD NOT SHORTENED THE SIEGE AND RESTRAINED THE ROMANS, THEY WOULD HAVE EXTERMINATED THE JEWISH.

THE LAST DAY'S

WALKING IN THE PRESENCES OF GOD MOVING BUILDING A KINGDOM SYSTEM TO HELP OTHERS ADVANCE FORWARD IN A PURPOSEFUL LIFESTYLE IT'S PART OF MY GOD'S GIVEN ASSIGNMENT WOW! WHEN THE WORLD IS UPON YOUR SHOULDER'S SUCH HUGE RESPONSIBILITY I MUST SAY.

PSALM 23:1-2-3-4-5-6 THE LORD IS MY SHEPHERED; I SHALL NOT WANT.

23:2 HE MAKETH ME TO LIE DOWN IN GREEN PASTURES: HE LEADETH ME BESIDE THE STILL WATERS.

23:3 HE RESTORETH MY SOUL: HE LEADETH ME IN THE PATH OF RIGHTEOUSNESS FOR HIS NAME'S SAKE.

23:4 YEA, THOUGH I WALK THROUGH THE VALLEY OF THE SHADOW OF DEATH, I WILL FEAR NO EVIL: FOR THOU ART WITH ME; THY ROD AND THY STAFF THEY COMFORTH ME.

23:5 THOU PREPAREST A TABLE BEFORE ME IN THE PRESENCE OF MINE ENEMIES: THOU ANOINTEST MY HEAD WITH OIL; MY CUP RUNNETH OVER.

23:6 SURELY GOODNESS AND MERCY SHALL FOLLOW ME ALL THE DAYS OF MY LIFE: AND I WILL DWELL IN THE HOUSE OF THE LORD FOR EVER.

ISAIAH 48:22 THERE IS NO PEACE, SAITH THE LORD, UNTO THE WICKED.

A RANDOM ACT OF KINDNESS

UNEXPECTED ACT OF CHARITY OR HELPFULNESS IS OFTEN DONE FOR A STRANGER ON THIS PARTICULAR DAY APRIL 04, 2022 BEHOLD A STRANGE UNEXPECTED KNOCK AT THE DOOR POST THIS MORNING BETWEEN THE HOUR OF 7:30 am I LOOK OUT THE PEEP HOLE I THEN PROCEEDED TO OPEN IT THERE APPEARED TWO YOUNG MEN ONE BEGIN EXPLAINING HIS CONDITION, HE WAS STANDING WITH BLOOD FLOWING FROM HIS NOISE NEXT MY FIRST REACTIONS TO START IMMEDIATELY ASSISTING HIM WITH FIRST AID MOREOVER THEN SUDDENLY I BEGAN TAKEN AUTHORITY BY SUPPLICATION, DECREEING DECLARING REQUESTING FOR THIS I'LLNESS TO COME INTO ORDER BY BOWING DOWN UNDER SUBJECTION WITH THE POWER OF HOLY ANOINTING FROM THE PRECIOUS BLOOD JESUS CHRIST.

WOW! WHAT A SURPRISE I MUST SAY THIS YOUNG MAN'S NAME WAS CALEB, HIM AND HIS FRIEND WERE ON THEIR WAY HEADING OUT TO SCHOOL NOW LET'S PAUSE FOR A BRIEF MOMENT. THESE TWO INDIVIDUALS HAD ALL OPPORTUNITY TO STOP AT MY NEIGHBORS DOOR OR ANY OTHER DOOR POST IN THE AREA INADD-ITION THIS IS'NT A COINCIDENT, ACCIDENT SUDDENLY THAT OCCURRED AT THIS VERY HOUR AS RESULTING ABOUT THE ISSUES OF BLOOD OKAY I'VE FINISHED HELPING RESOLVING CALEB

PROBLEM. BESIDES FROM THAT EPISODE I PROCEEDED ON ABRUPTLY SOON AFTER MY GRAND DAUGHTER NOSE STARTED TO BLEED MYSTERIOUSLY AS WELL WOW! NOW TYPICALLY, SHE DOES'NT USUALLY HAVE THIS TYPE BLOOD ISSUES. I PERSONALLY TRULY BELIEVE THIS A SET UP BY THE EVIL DARK FORCES TRYING TO OPPOSED; MY FINAL IN LAST DAY OF SLAYING THE DEVIL AND HIS AGENTS DESTROYING BREAKING PULLING DOWN EVERY STRONG-HOLDS. THIS OUR HOUR ENTERING INTO THE PROMISED LAND I'AM VICTORIOUS COURAGEOUS STRONG AND MIGHTY IN BATTLES WHO'S DEFEATING OVER THROWING HAMANS ATTACKS FOR SUCH A TIME AS THIS

"A TIME OF TROUBLE"

THIS THE HOUR FOR PASSOVER SEASON WE'RE CROSSING OVER THE RED SEA I'AM PUZZLE WAS THIS ACT BY THE HAND OF GOD?

"A PLEA FOR THE PEOPLE"

NUMBERS 13:30 AND CALEB STILLED THE PEOPLE BEFORE MOSES, AND SAID LET US GO UP AT ONCE, AND POSSES IT, FOR WE ARE WELL ABLE TO OVERCOME IT.

WE'RE STILL RAGGING WITH WARFARE BATTLES IN THIS SEASON FOR THE UNSEEN SUPERNATURAL REALM I'AM LITERALLY SPEAKING FROM SPIRITUAL POINT OF VIEW. GOD'S MIGHTY ARMY AT WORK BEHIND THE SCENES NO EVIL SPELLS OR WICKED PLOTS WILL PREVAIL OVER GOD PLANS.

GIVEN PRAISE AN HONOR'S GLORIFYING YESHUA HAMAS

HIACH THERE'S A BIG PROMOTION CELEBRATION AN IMPORTANT CURRENT EVENT'S UNFOLDING TAKEN PLACE WORLDWIDE IN THIS MONTH OF APRIL GOD'S EXPOSING HIS TRUE PROPHETS END TIMES OF WORLD HISTORICAL UNPRECEDENTED ERA, THEREFORE BELOVED HUMBLE YOURSELVES UNDER THE ALMIGHTY HAND OF GOD, THAT HE MAY EXALT THEE IN WELL DUE TIME AND SEASONS.

THE HOUSE OF REFUGE SAFE HEAVEN SHELTER YOU'RE ALL WELCOME IN THE MIGHTY NAME OF YAHWEH OUR WONDERFUL COUNSELOR GUIDING OUR EVERY STEP'S AND BY THIS ACTION A MULTITUDE ARE SAVED GOD'S CHOSEN ONES ARE RESPONSIBLE TO AWAKEN THEIR BROTHER'S AND SISTER'S

"GOD'S MIGHTY FAITHFUL SERVANT'S"

"A FAITHFUL SOLIDER THOU ART MERCIFUL"

FRUIT OF THE SPIRIT A RANDOM ACT OF LOVE AND KINDNESS.

"LISTEN TO A PARABLE"

GALATIAN 5:22 BUT THE FRUIT OF THE SPIRIT IS LOVE, JOY, PEACE, FOR BEARANCE, KINDNESS, GOODNESS, FAITHFULNESS, GENTLNESS, AND SELF CONTROL AGAINST SUCH THINGS.

"JESUS IS WORTHY OF OUR PRAISE"

TRANSMITTING CONNECTION THROUGH TELEPATIC TOUCH THOUGHTS.

TELECOMMUNICATIONS THROUGH SPIRITUAL CONVERSATIONS BEHOLD ON THIS PARTICULAR DAY APRIL 07, 2022 MY OLDIEST GRAND DAUGHTER APPROACH ME THEN ASK IF SHE CAN CALL HER AUNTIE IMMEDIATELY I REPLY SURE YOU MAY, MEAN WHILE WE'RE OUT IN ABOUT LET'S PAUSE FOR A SECOND OR TWO NOW REMIND YOU SHE HAS'NT SPOKEN TO HER AUNTIE FOR NEARLY TWO MONTHS. WELL IT WAS SURELY TIME TO HEAD BACK HOME SO THEREFORE IN THE MEAN TIME WHILE CONNECTING THE WIRE BACK INTO THE PHONE GUEST WHAT? BREAKING NEWS COMETH FORTH OUT OF NO WHERE SUDDENLY THE PHONE STARTED TO RING WOW AN WOW! LOOK AT THE MOVE OF GOD'S HANDS TOUCHING THAT SPEED DIAL. SUCH A POWERFUL AWESOME, AMAZING MYSTERIOUS DIVINE PROPHETIC HOOK UP!

THE HOLY ANGELS DELIBERATELY ASSIST US THROUGH SPIRITUAL TELECOMMUNICATION TO HELP TRANSLATE OUR DIVINE CONVERSATIONS BY REVEALING THE MARACULOUS SUPERPOWER AND ENERGY OF GOD'S SECERT MYSTERIES.

I'AM GRATEFUL, THANKFUL TO PARTICIPATE BY RECEIVING OR EXPERIENCING SUCH HIGH LEVELS TO RECORD THESE AMAZING, FASCINATING, REMARKABLE DYNAMIC, AND DUNAMIS SUPRENATURAL POWER GIVEN THE MESSAGES THROUGH AIRWAVES FREQUENCY ENERGY CONNECTING WITH OUR HIGHER SOURCE THAT'S WHAT YOU WILL CALL OPERATING IN AUTHORITY KNOWLEDGE AND WISDOM THIS TYPE OF SKILLS ACQUIRED SPIRITUAL UNDERSTANDING ANYONE CAN HAVE ACCESS BUT ARE YOU WILLING TO EXCEPT JESUS CHRIST AS YOUR LORD SAVIOR AND SUBMIT REPENT CHANGE FROM YOUR EVIL WICKED WAY'S. THEN HE WILL HEAR FROM EACH ONE OF YOUR SUPPLICATIONS JUST RENDER YOUR HEARTS OVER TO OUR ALMIGHTY ABBA FATHER HE'S WAITING HE TRULY LOVE'S ALL HUMANITY. ONLY IF YOU CAN IMAGINE THIS JOY IS THE INFALLIBLE, INVISIBLE AND TANGIBLE SIGN OF THE PRESENCE OF GOD'S GLORY.

A MARRIAGE CEREMONY CELEBRATION THEN SUDDENLY DEATH OCCURRED Pt. 2

BEHOLD ON THIS SPECIAL, SPECTACULAR AND WONDERFUL WEDDING EVENT TAKEN PLACE TODAY APRIL 16, 2022 THIS VERY EXCITING BEAUTIFUL MOMENT. I'LL MENTION ABOUT MY BROTHER IN-LAW THE BRIDE AN GROOM WHICH IS MY NIECE AND NEPHEW IN-LAW LET'S PAUSE THIS FILM FOR JUST A FEW SECOND HERE. NOW I'AM GOING TO LITERALLY TRAVEL BACK INTO THE PAST TIME, SPACE ACTUALLY WE'RE TALKING ABOUT A TIME ZONE FIVE MONTHS AGO ON THIS DAY OF DECEMBER 25, 2021 I'VE RECEIVED A NIGHT VISITATION IN REFERENCING TO THIS HORRIFYING, SHOCKING UNPLEASEANT ENCOUNTER BASED UPON THE DEATH OF MY BROTHER IN-LAW NOW REMIND YOU THIS COURSE OF ACTION WAS EXTREMELY TAKEN PLACE IN THE SUPERNATURAL REALM WORKING BEHIND SCENE SIGNIFICALLY OBSERVING THROUGH SPIRITUAL LEN'S WOW! SUCH HEAVY POWERFUL DOWNLOADS FROM A SPIRITUAL POINT OF VIEW. NONETHELESS ALLUDES TO THE UNSEEN GAZING OUT OF SIGHT OVER INTO THE SPOOKY THIRD DIMENSION MOREOVER MY BROTHER IN-LAW DEVELOPED AND BATTLE FROM A RARE FORM OF DISEASE, SO THEREFORE THE STATE OF HIS CONDITION CIRCUMSTANCES PROGNOSIS PROGRESSIVELY WORSE'N BESIDES FROM THAT THE BIGGEST, WISH FROM MY NIECE

AN EVERYONE ELSE WAS BELIEVING HOPING PRAYING ANTICIPATING AND LOOKING FORWARD WITH THE BRIDE'S REQUEST TO BE FULFILLED. LONG STORY SHORT TRADITIONALLY FATHER'S ARE SUPPOSEDLY TO ENGAGE OR INVOLVE THEMSELVES BY WALKING THEIR DAUGHTER'S DOWN THE AISLES WITH THAT BEING SAID.

HOWEVER NEXT ACTION LET'S ROLL THIS FILM FORWARD FIVE MONTHS LATER LEADING UP TO THIS DAY APRIL 16, 2022 SUCH A GREAT SPECIAL OCCASION TAKEN PLACE ONCE AGAIN RECORDING IN TIME HISTORY EVERTHING IN MOTION; EVERYONE STARTS TO ARRIVE EACH ONE GREETING THEMSELVES MEAN WHILE AT THIS POINT IT WAS DEFINITELY TIME FOR THE CEREMONY TO BEGIN LIGHT'S, CAMERA AND ACTION NONETHELESS MY NIECE HAS EMBRACED HERSELF FOR THIS VERY SPECIAL OCCASION DUE TO THE FACT OF HER FATHER'S MEDICAL CONDITIONS AND LIMITATIONS WHICH HOWEVER ALLOWED HIM TO AIMED VIGOROUS AN DETERMINED BY EVERY ATTEMPTS FULFILLING HIS OBLIGATION WITH THE MAXIMUM STRUGGLE AN EXERTION OF HIS FULL CAPACITY STRENGTH. NOT KNOWING IN THIS VERY FINAL HOUR THIS WOULD BE HIS LAST FINAL ATTEMPT TO WALK HEAR ON EARTH; LET'S PAUSE FOR A BRIEF MOMENT HERE TO BE CONTINUE. NOT EVEN AN HOUR LATER SHOCKING BREAKING NEW'S SUDDENLY QUICKLY, IMMEDIATELY AND UNEXPECTEDLY HE PASSED AWAY AT ONCE INSTANTANEOUSLY SOON AFTER LET'S SAY BETWEEN THE DURATION THE TIME OF HIS TRANSITION WHICH OCCURRED MOREOVER HIS YOUNGEST DAUGHTER AND I HAD A DEEP CONVERSATION, SHE THEN SHARED WITH ME ABOUT THIS NIGHT VISITATION OF A DREAM SHE PREVOUSLY ENCOUNTER PRIOR UPON THE ARRIVAL ABOUT HER FATHER'S DEATH. WOW! I'M TOTALLY BLOWN AWAY COULD'NT BELIEVE AT

THIS POINT THAT OUR SUPEME MIGHTY SOVEREIGNITY REDEEMER HAS DOWNLOADED REVELATION INTO OUR SPIRIT MAN THE EXACT PRECISE SOME WHAT DIFFERENT IN DETAILS. I STOP AND PAUSE FOR A FEW MINUTES I THEN PROCEED ON SHARING BY EXPLAINING TO HER MY PRIOR PREVOIUS NIGHT VISITATION REVELATION ABOUT THEIR DEAR BELOVED FATHER. I'AM IN SHOCK FOR THE MOST PART AND FEELING SAD, HEART BROKEN DEVASTING EMOTIONALLY, OVERWHELMED WITH THIS SUDDENT TRAGEDY SORROW'S GRIEF AND MOURNING.

SUCH A BEAUTIFUL!

"BRIDE & GROOM"

"IN HIS PRESENCES"

DEATH, BURIAL AND RESURRECTION CROSSING OVER INTO ETERNAL EVERLASTING EXISTENCE, TO BE ABSENT FROM THE BODY AND TO BE CAUGHT UP IN THE PRESENCES OF GOD GLORY!

"A NIGHT TO REMEMBER"

WHAT A PICTURE PHOTOGRAPHIC MEMORIES CELEBRATING SPECIAL SEASON PASSOVER FOR THE PASSION OF JESUS CHRIST FROM NAZARETH A WEDDING FEAST AND THE HOMEGOING OF OUR DEAR BELOVED WE'LL BE TOUCH ON THIS DAY HE DEFINITELY RAN HIS COURSE AND RACE WITH GREAT PETIENCE TO ENDURED TO THE VERY END NO MORE WORRIES SUFFERING AND PAIN.

LOVE YOU BELOVED!

REST IN PEACE

BROTHER IN-LAW

JANUARY 04, 1965

APRIL 16,2022

"I WILL POUR OUT MY SPIRIT UPON ALL FLESH"

JOEL 2:27-28 AND YE SHALL KNOW THAT I AM IN THE MIST OF ISRAEL, AND THAT I AM THE LORD YOUR GOD, AND NONE ELSE: AND MY PEOPLE SHALL NEVER BE ASHAMED.

2:28 AND IT SHALL COME TO PASS AFTER WORD, THAT I WILL POUR OUT MY SPIRIT UPON ALL FLESH; AND YOUR SONS AND DAUGHTERS SHALL PROPHESY, YOUR OLD MEN SHALL DREAM DREAMS YOUR YOUNG MEN SHALL SEE VISIONS:

SEEING IN THE NATURAL VS SEE IN THE SUPERNATURAL

DO YOU KNOW THE SECRET'S SECURITY CODE'S TO THE MASTER MIND VAULT?

IT ALL START'S WITH A SINGLE THOUGHT BY CREATING SOMETHING INTO EXISTENCE FROM A STATE OF BEYOND DARKNESS TO ENTER A MAGNIFICENT LIMITLESS LIFE WORLD ADVENTURE'S THAT EASLEY AWAITS YOU WHILE EXPERIENCING A DIVINELY MARVELOUS SPLENDID EXTRAORDINARY ILLUMINATION FROM WITHIN MAN'S TEMPLE.

"GOD'S WISDOM"

1. WHAT ARE GOD'S MYSTERIES?

   CONFIRMATION, CONFESSION, REPENTANCE RECONCILIATION HOLY COMMINION HOLY MATRIMONY ORDINATION HOLY ORDER AND, UNCTION.

2. WHAT ARE THE MYSTERIES OF THE KINGDOM OF GOD?

   WE MUST BE CHOSEN BY GOD AND IS CALLED OUT OF HIS MISCHIEVOUS CHILDHOOD TO PARTAKE IN

THE KINGDOM OF GOD. YOU MUST GO THROUGH TRAILS, TESTS AND SPIRITUAL WARFARE, BEFORE THE MYSTERY UNFOLDS AND BECOME EXPOSED.

3. HOW DO YOU KNOW YOU ARE CHOSEN FROM GOD?

YOU MUST ACCEPT GOD'S FREE GIFT OF SALVATION, THEREFORE, IF YOU HAVE FULLY PUT YOUR TRUST IN HIM TO BE YOUR LORD AND SAVIOR, YOU ARE DEFINIELY CHOSEN.

4. IS EVERYONE CHOSEN BY GOD?

TITUS 1:1 PAUL, A SERVANT OF GOD, AND AN APOSTLE OF JESUS CHRIST, ACCORDING TO THE FAITH OF GOD'S ELECT, AND THE ACKNOWLEDGING OF THE TRUTH WHICH IS AFTER GODLINEESS.

5. WHO DOES GOD REVEAL HIS MYSTERIES TO?

AMOS 3:7 SURELY THE LORD GOD WILL DO NOTHING BUT HE REVEALETH HIS SECRET UNTO HIS SERVANTS THE PROPHETS.

6. HOW DO YOU KNOW WHEN GOD'S TRYING TO CONVEY OR TELL YOU SOMETHING?

    A. THROUGH REPETITIVE INSTRUCTION'S DIVINE DOWNLOAD MESSAGES

    B. THROUGH DREAMS NIGHTVISITATION INFORMATION REGARDS SPECIFICATION IMPARTING REVELATIONS

C. THROUGH A SMALL STILL VOICE OR PERHAPS A PROPHETIC MESSAGE THROUGH HIS PROPHETS

D. THROUGH SIGNS, SYMBOLS NUMBER'S MIRACULOUS HEALING AND WONDER'S.

7. WHAT POWERS DO THE CHOSEN ONES HAVE?

SPECIAL POWERS MIMIC BESTOWED POWER FROM SACRED ANESTOR. THE NIGHT REALITY WARPING, OR OTHER SPECIAL ABILITIES THAT PUT THEM IN A LEAGUE OF THEIR OWN.

"POWER OF WORD'S"

THE MYSTERY WHICH THEREFORE HAS BEEN HIDDEN FROM AGES AND THROUGHOUT GENERATIONS OFTEN TIME IT HAS ALSO REVEALED BUT GOD CAN USE ORDINARY PEOPLE TO DO SOME AWESOME, UNIQUE DISTINCTIVE EXTRAVAGANT AND SUPER-POWERFUL AMAZING THINGS.

WHAT IS A PERSON WHO SEES THE FUTURE CALLED?

A VISIONARY IS SOMEONE WITH A STRONG VISION OF THE FUTURE. SINCE VISIONS AREN'T ALL WAYS ACCURATE, A VISIONARY'S IDEAS MAY WORK BRILLIANTLY OR FAIL MISERABLY EVEN SO, VISIONARY IS USUALLY A POSTIVE WORD.

"WALKEN IN THE ILLUMINATION OF HIS GLORY"

1 CORINTHIANS 2:4-5-7 AND MY SPEECH AN MY PREACHING WAS NOT WITH ENTICING WORDS OF MAN'S WISDOM, BUT IN DEMONSTRATION OF THE SPIRIT AND OF POWER:

2:5 THAT YOUR FAITH SHOULD NOT STAND IN THE WISDOM OF MEN, BUT IN THE POWER OF GOD.

2:7 BUT WE SPEAK THE WISDOM OF GOD IN A MYSTERY, EVEN THE HIDDEN WISDOM. WHICH GOD

ORDAINED BEFORE THE WORLD UNTO OUR GLORY:

LUKE 8:10 AND HE SAID, UNTO YOU IT IS GIVEN TO KNOW THE MYSTERIES OF THE KINGDOM OF GOD: BUT TO OTHERS IN PARABLES; THAT SEEING THEY MIGHT NOT SEE, AND HEARING THEY MIGHT NOT UNDERSTAND.

JOB 33:15-16-17-18 IN A DREAM, IN A VISION OF NIGHT, WHEN DEEP SLEEP FALLETH UPON MEN, IN SLUMERINGS UPON THE BED.

33:16 THEN HE OPENETH THE EARS OF MEN, AND SEALETH THEIR INSTRUCTIONS.

33:17 THAT HE MAY WITHDRAW MAN FROM HIS PURPOSE, AND HIDE PRIDE FROM MAN.

33:18 HE KEEPETH BACK HIS SOUL FROM THE PIT, AND HIS LIFE FROM PERISHING BY THE SWORD.

ORDER MY STEPS IN THY WORD

ACTS 9:15-16 BUT THE LORD SAID UNTO HIM, GO THY WAY: FOR HE IS A CHOSEN VESSEL UNTO ME, TO BEAR MY NAME BEFORE THE GENTILES, AND KINGS AND THE CHILDREN OF ISRAEL:

9:16 FOR I WILL SHEW HIM HOW GREAT THINGS HE MUST SUFFER FOR MY NAME'S SAKE.

JEREMIAH 33:3-5 CALL UNTO ME, AND I WILL ANSWER THEE, AND SHOW THEE GREAT AND MIGHTY THINGS, WHICH THOU KNOWEST NOT.

JEREMIAH 1:5 BEFORE I FORMED THEE IN THE BELLY I KNEW THEE, AND BEFORE THOU CAMEST FORTH OUT OF THE WOMB I SANCTIFIED THEE, AND I ORDAINED THEE A PROPHET UNTO THE NATIONS

JEREMIAH 29:11 FOR I KNOW THE THOUGHTS THAT I THINK TOWARDS YOU, SAITH THE LORD, THOUGHTS OF PEACE, AND NOT OF EVIL, TO GIVE YOU AN EXPECTED END.

"YE ARE MY WITENESSES"
CALLED TO DUTY

    A. CO-CREATOR'S
    B. CALLED

C. CHOSEN

D. COMMISSION

MATTHEW 22:14 FOR MANY ARE CALLED, BUT FEW ARE CHOSEN.

ELEVATING MAN'S IQ TO A HIGHER POSITION BY STIMULATING, ACTIVATING, PROCESSING AND DEVELOPING HIS GROWTH SYSTEM TO A HIGHER VOLUME FREQUENCY VIBRATION LEVEL WERE THE HUMAN BRAIN CAN ARRIVE AT IT'S RESTING STATE WHICH CALLED WHO AM'I MY FATHER AND I BECOME ONENESS WHAT SOEVER AS A MAN THINK IT IN HIS MIND AND HEART SO SHALL THE ISSUES OF HIS LIFE FLOWS FROM HIS BELLY.

"HELP MINE UNBELIEF ANCIENT ONE CREATE ME A NEW HEART"

MEN'S HEARTS FAILING THEM FROM OUT OF FEAR

THERE'S EVIDENCED STATING THAT VIOLENCE ATROCITIES, WARS, FAMINE, DEVASTATION, AND DESTRUCTIVE FORCES OF NATURE REPORT BY THE MEDIA EACH DAY. WE'RE MOST CERTAINLY AND OBVIOUSLY LIVING IN THE GREAT TIME OF MASSIVE CONFUSION OVERWHELMED WITH GRIEF MALICE, HATRED, JEALOUS AND UNREPENTING SIN.

BIBLICAL PREDICTIONS, PROPHECY BY THE LORD WHEN HE SAID. "AND IN THAT DAY THE WHOLE EARTH SHALL BE IN COMMOTION AND MEN'S HEARTS SHALL FAIL THEM"

MEN'S HEART'S ARE FAILING AND THAT INCLUDES WOMEN BECAUSE THEY FORGET THEIR IDENTITY AND THEIR PURPOSE HAVING OUR "HEARTS FAIL US "IT MEANS THAT WE LOSE OUR FAITH AND BELIEF THAT THING WILL GET BETTER. PRESIDENT NELSON TEACHES US THAT WE SPECIFICALLY LOSE OUR FAITH WHEN WE DO TWO THINGS FORGOT OUR IDENTITY WHO AM I?

"UNREPENTING SIN"

PSALMS 97:10 LET THOSE WHO LOVE THE LORD HATE EVIL, FOR HE GUARDS THE LIVES OF HIS FAITHFUL ONES AND DELIVERS THEM FROM THE HAND OF THE WICKED.

PALMS 101:6-7 MINE EYE'S SHALL BE UPON THE FAITHFUL OF THE LAND, THAT THEY MAY DWELL WITH ME: HE THAT WALKETH IN A PERFECT WAY, HE SHALL SERVE ME.

101:7 HE THAT WORKETH DECIET SHALL NOT DWELL WITHIN MY HOUSE: HE THAT TELLETH LIES SHALL NOT TARRY IN MY SIGHT.

MAN'S MASTERING HIS OWN TOUGHTS WAYS CONDITION AND EMOTIONS BY SIMPLY NOT OBEYING GOD

THERE'S SEVEN EASY FUNDAMENTAL, DEVELOPMENT FORMULA AN CURRICULUM IT'S A NECESSARY BASE SYSTEMATIC, ASSESSMENT TO REVIEW AT A SCHOOL LEVEL OR COLLEGE EDUCATIONAL LEARNING COURSE OF STUDIES ONCE MAN APPLIED AND PRACTICE THESE SEVEN SET OF SKILLS BY ACQUIRING ANALYZING HIS BEHAVIOR THOUGHTS PATTERING DUE TO LACK OF LOW IQ DEFICIENCIES WTHIN HIS OR HER OWN CONSCIOUSNESS STATE OF MIND. MAN'S FINAL ACADEMIC, ACHIEVEMENTS WITH GREAT EXCELLENCE TO ACCELERATE, CATAPULT HIM OR HER INTO ADVANCING FORWARD TO A MORAL

COGNITIVE DIVINE INTELLECTUAL HIGH RANKING PRODUCTIVE BEHAVIOR STATUS THERE'S LESSON'S AND TEST'S WE ALL MUST PASS IN ORDER TO EXCEL AT THE LEVEL OF A MYSTERY MIND'S MASTER'S PROGRAM.

ADVISE TO YOUNG MEN AND WOMEN Y'ALL WELL INFORMED LAWS OF ACTION, KEEP GOD'S UNIVERSAL LAW'S AND PRINCIPLES WATCH IT WORK

1. PUT ASIDE PRIDE

2. STAY FAITHFUL, SILENT AND HUMBLE

3. GETTING GOD'S WISDOM AND UNDERSTANDING

WHAT ARE THE 7 HEALTHY CONSCIOUSNESS TIPS

1. I'AM CONSCIOUSNESS

2. POINT OF VIEW

3. THE UNCONSCIOUS-BELIEFS

4. THE SUBCONSICIOUS-FEELINGS

5. THE CONSCIOUS MIND/THOUGHTS

6. THE POWER OF CHANGE YOUR REALITY

7. MAN'S MIND IS LIKE A VEHICLE TRANSPORTING DATA INFROMATION FROM DIFFERENT DIMENSION OR LOCATIONS TRAVELING IN THE KNOWN OR THE UNKNOWN SUPERNATURAL WORLD

DO YOU KNOW THE SECRET DNA SECURITY CODES?

WHAT DOES DNA MEANS? ADOPTED IN A ROYAL BLOOD LINE COVENANT

A. D- DEITY OF THE FATHER'S OFFSPRING DIVINE DIVINITY BLOOD LINE

B. N- NOT NORMAL DESCRIBES, CONDITION BEHAVIOR AND UNUSUAL DIFFERENT A TYPICAL NEGATIVE BELIEF SYSTEM SUCH AS NAÏVE, NASTY, NARCISSISTIC, NAUGHTY, AND NEFARIOUS BLOOD TRAITS CROSSING OVER INTO A NEW BORN BLOOD BOUGHT TRANSFUSION COVENANT WITH THE HEAVENLY FATHER'S INHERITANCE

C. A- ALIGNMENT, ATTAINING, ACCOMPLISING BY EXPRESSING CHARACTERISTIC OR ATTRIBUTES LIKE OUR FATHER'S DNA

THE POWER OF THE BLOOD COVENANT BETWEEN GOD AND EVERY BELIEVER IS SEALED WITH THE BLOOD OF JESUS CHRIST

AN APPROPRIATE APPOINTED TIME WHEN THRONS IN YOUR SIDES

ECCLESIASTES 1:18 FOR IN MUCH WISDOM IS MUCH GRIEF: AND HE THAT INCREASETH KNOWLEDGE INCREASETH SORROW.

3:1 TO EVERYTHING THERE IS A SEASON, AND A TIME TO EVERY PURPOSE UNDER THE HEAVEN:

3:2 A TIME TO BE BORN, AND A TIME TO DIE; A TIME TO PLANT, AND A TIME TO PLUCK UP THAT WHICH IS PLANTED;

3:3 A TIME TO KILL, AND A TIME TO HEAL; A TIME TO BREAK DOWN, AND A TIME TO BUILD UP;

3:4 A TIME TO WEEP, AND A TIME TO LAUGH; A TIME TO MOURN, AND A TIME TO DANCE;

3:5 A TIME TO CAST AWAY STONES, AND A TIME TO GATHER STONES TOGETHER; A TIME TO EMBRACE, AND A TIME TO REFRAIN FROM EMBRACING.

3:6 A TIME TO GET, AND A TIME TO LOSE; A TIME TO KEEP, AND A TIME TO CAST AWAY;

3:7 A TIME TO REND, AND A TIME TO SEW; A TIME. TO KEEP SILENCE; AND A TIME TO SPEAK

3:8 A TIME TO LOVE, AND A TIME TO HATE; A TIME TO WAR, AND A TIME OF PEACE.

3:12 I KNOW THAT THERE IS NO GOOD IN THEM, BUT FOR A MAN TO REJOICE, AND TO DO GOOD IN HIS LIFE.

3:13 AND ALSO THAT EVERY MAN SHOULD EAT AND DRINK, AND ENJOY THE GOOD OF ALL HIS LABOUR, IT IS THE GIFT OF GOD

ECCLESIASTES 4:9 TWO ARE BETTER THAN ONE; BECAUSE THEY HAVE A GOOD REWARD OF THEIR LABOUR.

4:10 FOR IF THEY FALL, THE ONE WILL LIFT UP HIS FELLOW: BUT WOE TO HIM THAT IS ALONE WHEN HE FALLETH; FOR HE HATH NOT ANOTHER TO HELP HIM UP.

WHAT ARE THE THRONS IN OUR LIVES?

WHEN PEOPLE SPEAKS ABOUT THRONS IN THE FLESH, WE'RE REFERRING TO MANY LIFE'S CHALLENGES AND STRUGGLES, AFFLICTIONS PERSECUTION THAT, WHICH WE EITHER LIVE WITH OR ENDURE FOR A CERTAIN PERIOD OF TIME.

BEHOLD WHAT IN THE WORLD IS GOING ON LORD

I WOKE UP ON THIS DAY SEPTEMBER 11, 2022 AT APPROXIMATELY 5:00am I PROCEEDED TO GO GET READY BY BRUSHING MY TEETH I SOON REALIZE OR NOTICES SPITTING UP BLOOD HOWEVER I THEN SAID DEAR CHILD OF GOD A TIME OF TROUBLE HAS FALLEN UPON ME OR EITHER SOMEONE ELSE CLOSE INSPITE OF THE CIRCUMSTANCES HAPPENING AROUND ME IMMEDIATELY I BEGAN TO PRAY BY REQUESTING EARNESTLY SUPPLICATIONS AND PETITIONING ON THE BEHALF OF WHOM EVERY I'M SUPPOSE TO STAND IN THE GAP. FURTHEREMORE, I STARTED ASKING ABBA FATHER PLEASE REVEALED IT INADDITION I PROCEEDED ON MY THREE MILE WALK JOURENY HOUR'S LATER I RETURN HOME MY DAUGHTER CAME WITH THE BREAKING NEW'S ALERT. IT'S ABOUT HER DEAREST BEST FRIEND SHE'S LIKE A BELOVED DAUGHTER TO ME LET'S PAUSE FOR A BRIEF MOMENT OKAY LET'S MOVE FORWARD THIS YOUNG LADY HAD A MASSIVE STROKE AND SLIPPED INTO A COMA. FROM THAT POINT I BEGAN TO STAY IN THE WARROOM FOR PRAYER'S REQUESTING THAT SHE FIND FAVOR IN THE SIGHT OF GOD AND MAN BESIDES FROM THAT HER BRAIN WAS HEMORRHAGING BUT GUEST WHAT? THE DOTOR'S DID A TC SCAN EXAMINATION THREE DAY'S LATER ON SEPTMBER 14, 2022 SUDDENLY THE BLEEDING IMMEDIATELY STOP LOOK AT THE HAND OF GOD MOVE

SWIFTLY AND SPEEDYLY NOW REMIND YA'LL SHE'S STILL ASLEEP YOU TALKING ABOUT SOMEONE CALLING FORTH COMMANDING HER GUARDING, NURSE ANGEL'S TO STAND AND SLAY ANY EVIL ENTITY BY HOLDING THAT OLD DEATH ANGEL BACK BECAREFUL BECAUSE THE ADVERSARY OUT SEEKING WHOM HE CAN DEVOUR IN THIS DARK FINAL END TIMES OF HOUR'S NO WEAPON THAT FORMED AGAINST HER SHALL NOT PROSPER WE'RE ALL PRAYING FOR THE PRECIOUS BLOOD OF OUR HOLY LAMB GIVE HER A SECOND CHANCE. STAY TUNE FOR THE NEXT EPISODE TO BE

CONTINUE Pt. 1

FLORIDA TROPICAL CYCLONE HURRICANE CATASTROPHICA DISASTER

GOD FOREWARN BEFOREHAND ABOUT BACK IN 2009 APPROXIMATELY FOURTEEN YEAR'S AGO THE HOLY OF HOLIEST SPIRIT CAME TO ME IN A NIGHT VISITATION HE SHOWED ME ABOUT THE STATE OF FLORIDA LET'S PAUSE FOR A BREIF MOMENT OKAY WER'RE MOVING FORWARD NOW INTO THIS DREAM. WHILE EXPERIENCING LOOKING FOR SOME REAL ESTATE PROPERTY TO PURCHASE CAN YOU IMAGINE IT WAS A NICE BEAUTIFUL SUNNY DAY. NEVERTHELESS I STOP AND PAUSE FOR A MINUTE THEN QUESTION THE REALTOR AGENT ABOUT FLORIDA HAVING CREEPING CREATURES SUCH AS ALLIGATOR'S, AND CROCODILES JUST FREELY WONDERING, LURKING THROUGH THE NEIGHBORHOOD HOWEVER I MUST MENTION THAT THIS WAS THE VERY FIRST ENCOUNTER WHICH GOD DOWNLOADED INTO MY SPIRIT MAN. NOW STAY TUNE THIS EPISODE TO BE CONTINUE Pt.1 BREAKING NEW'S ALERT SEVERAL MONTH'S LATER GOD APPEARED ONCE AGAIN FOR THE SECOND TIME SHOWING ME THE STATE OF FLORIDA. NOW REMIND YA'LL I NEVER UNDERSTOOD THE REVELATION ACCORDING THESE MESSAGE I'VE PERSONALY DISREGARD AND IGNORED ALL TELL, TALE SIGNS BY PUTTING THOSE TWO DREAMS BACK UPON THE SHELVES NOW THIS IS PART# 2 NOW

ALWAYS REMEMBER GOD DOES COME COMMUNICATE BY FORETELLING SOUNDING THE ALARM TO HIS CHILDREN'S OR PROPHETS AMONGST THE PEOPLE FIRSTHAND I DID'NT EVEN KNOW HOW TO INTERPRET THE VISION'S WOW! UNTIL FOURTEEN YEARS' LATER ONCE AGAIN BREAKING NEW'S REPORT Pt. 3 WHO COULD'VE ONLY IMAGINE ON THIS DAY SEPTEMBER 23, 2022 ONE OF LIFES HUGE ENORMOUS MOST POWERFUL CATASTROPHIC NATURAL DISASTER STORM TAKEN PLACE IT HAS CAUSE THE WALLS TO COLLAPES AND TRAGICALLY CLAIMED MANY LIVES. I'AM TRULY DEEPLY SADDENED FOR THE LOST OF OTHER'S AND THE ONES WHO HAVE TO MOURN WITH SUCH GRIEF I WILL CONTINUE TO STAY IN PRAYER FOR MY BROTHER'S AND SISTER'S INADDITION TO THAT HOWEVER I TRULY AND HONESTLY, HATE TO BE THE ONE WHO MUST BRING FORTH THIS MESSAGE I'AM COMING IN LOVE AS A SEER IN THIS FINAL HOUR. THE AXE HAS BEEN PUT TO THE ROOTS OUR EARTH, WORLD DEEPLY EXPERIENCING DEVASTATION CALAMITY AND TRAVILING PAINS ACROSS THE GLOBE DUE TO UNREPENTING EVIL SIN THAT HAS CAUSE MEN OR MANY TO SUFFER. OH! BUT GOD DOES HAVE THE LAST AND FINAL SAY IN THIS HOUR A GREAT AWAKEN HAS FALLEN UPON THE DEEP DEPTH EARTH, LAND AND SEA. IT'S A TOUCHY SUBJECT OR MATTER HERE, MY GOD GIVEN ASSIGNMENT TO COME BACK HELP MANKIND TO RESTORE THEIR HEART'S BY SURRENDERING, REPENTING BACK TO OUR HEAVENLY FATHER AND THEN HE WILL SURELY HEAL THE LAND.

I'AM PUBLICLY ANNOUNCING A FORMAL DECLARATION WITH ALL SINCERELY, SERIOUSLY AND PROPHETICALLY ON BEHALF OF ALL MANKIND.

"WALKEN IN THE FIELDS OF DRY BONE'S"

"LISTEN TO A PARABLE"

2 CHRONICLES 7:14 IF MY PEOPLE WHO ARE CALLED BY MY NAME, WILL HUMBLE THEMSELVES AND PRAY AND SEEK MY FACE AND TURN FROM THEIR WICKED WAYS, THEN I WILL HEAR FROM HEAVEN; AND I WILL FORGIVE THEIR SIN AND WILL HEAL THEIR LAND.

"I COME NOT TO CONDEMN THE WORLD BUT TO SAVE THE WORLD THROUGH HIM"

JOHN 3:16 FOR GOD SO LOVED THE WORLD, THAT HE GAVE HIS ONLY BEGOTTEN SON, THAT WHOSOEVER BELIEVETH IN HIM SHOULD NOT PERISH, BUT HAVE EVER LASTING LIFE.

3:17 FOR GOD SO LOVED THE WORLD THAT HE GAVE HIS ONE AND ONLY SON, THAT WHOEVER BELIEVES IN HIM SHALL NOT PERISH BUT HAVE ETERNAL LIFE. FOR GOD DID NOT SEND HIS SON INTO THE WORLD TO CONDEMN THE WORLD BUT TO SAVE THE WORLD THROUGH HIM.

THE LAST 444 FINAL CLARION CALL

OCTOBER 1,2022 ON THIS EARLY MORNING JOURENY WHILE TAKEN A NORMAL ROUTINE WALK APPROXIMATELY BETWEEN 3 TO 4 MILES STRETCH MOREOVER PERHAPS AT THE VERY MOMENT I LOOKED UP BEHOLD THERE GOES FOUR BIRD'S FLYING RIGHT IN FRONT OF MY PATH IF I COULD ONLY HAVE STRETCH AND REACH UP I WOULD'VE TOUCH THOSE BIRD'S THAT'S HOW CLOSE WOW! NOT EVEN TEN MINUTES GOES BY ANOTHER SET OF FOUR BIRD'S FLYING ONCE AGAIN MOREOVER SHORTLY SOON AFTER BEFORE MY FINAL STRETCH LORD BEHOLD IMMEDIATELY LOOKED DOWN ON THE GROUND WOW! THERE GOES FOUR PENNIES I THOUGHT TO MYSELF SHOULD I OR SHOULD'NT I PICK UP THOSE COINS THEN SUDDENLY MY GREATER INTUITION KICK IN AND SAID DON'T DISRESPECT THE MONEY 3 SET'S OF 444 ON THIS TRAIL IT'S PRETTY IMPRESSIVE TOTALLY AMAZING WHAT IS GOD TRYING TO CONVEY THE HOLY ANGEL'S DEFINITELY SPEAKING IN THIS FINAL VERY HOUR PAY ATTENTION TO SIGNS SYMBOLS, MIRACLES AND WONDEROUS ALONG YOUR LIFE'S JOURNEY

"PREACH THE WORD THERE'S POWER IN THIS HOUR"

2 TIMOTHY 1:11 WHERE UNTO I AM APPOINTED A PEACHER, AND AN APOSTLE AND A TEACHER OF THE GENTILES.

BEHOLD WHAT IN THE WORLD IS GOING ON LORD Pt. 2

INADDITION I'AM JUST AN INTERCESSORY PRAYER WARRIOR WHILE KNEELING IN THE MID-NIGHT HOUR INSIDE OF HEAVENLY THRONE'S COURTS ROOM ON OCTOBER 6,2022 WITH FERVENT INTENSITY, AND PASSIONATE DECREES DECLARATIONS AN PLEA COMMANDING, DISPATCHING THE HOLY ANGEL'S HELLO! WORLD A BREAKING NEW' REPORT ONCE AGAIN WHAT A SUPERPOWERFUL SURPRISE ON THE VERY NEXT DAY OCTOBER 7,2022 GUEST WHAT? EVERYONE THIS INDIVIDUAL WOKE UP AND RESURRECTED FROM HER TOMB JUST SHY OF A MONTH BEING IN A COMA WE GIVE ALL PRAISES, GLORY AND HONOR'S TO OUR SUPREME SOVEIGNTY REDEEMER DEMONSTRATING A PROPHETIC POWERFUL BLESSING IT'S TOTALLY AWESOME, AMAZING THERE'S STILL SIGNS WONDEROUS WORKING MIRACULOUS, HEALING PERFORMING IN TIME WORLD HISTORY. NOW REMEMBER I'AM JUST A MESSENGER, WITNESS WHO WIELD MY HEART BACK TO THE FATHER IN A TIME OF TROUBLE TAKE ACTION WITH A LEAP INTO FAITH WALKEN BY FAITH NOT BY SIGHT

"O MAJESTY CALMS THE STORM'S"

A SPOKEN WORD

ACTS 1:8 BUT YOU WILL RECEIVE POWER WHEN THE HOLY SPIRIT COME ON YOU, AND YOU WILL BE MY WITNESSES IN JERUSALEM, AND IN ALL JUDEA AND SAMARIA, AND TO THE END OF THE EARTH.

STAY TUNE FOR THE NEXT EPISODE TO BE CONTINUE

A PROPHECY AN PREDICTION FROM A FOUR-YEAR-OLD BABE WOW!

GOOD MORNING AMERICA, I COME TO Y'ALL IN THE NAME OF YESHUA HAMASHIACH ON THIS DAY OCTOBER 17,2022 WITH ANOTHER PROPHETIC WORD MOREOVER THIS PROPHECY WAS SPOKEN FROM THE MOUTH OF MY 4YR OLD GRAND-DAUGHTER LET'S HEAR THE BREAKING NEW'S REPORT TO ME FROM THE DIVINE DOWNLOAD REVELATION, NOW REMIND YOU THIS REVELATION IS COMING FROM THE MOUTH OF A LITTLE BABE HER EXACT WORD'S GRANDMA' YOU'RE LIKE PRINCESS TIANA WHO WORKS HARD. INFACT, SHE WENT ON TO SAY YOU LOOK JUST LIKE HER INADDITION SHE CONTINUED ON SAYING I'AM GOING TO EVENTUALLY HAVE THE PRIVILEGE TO MEET MY PRINCE JUST LIKE TIANA I STOP AND PAUSED FOR A SECOND AND STARTED TO PONDER WOW! AND WOW! IF YOU COULD ONLY IMAGINE WHAT IT WILL FEEL LIKE IN SPITE OF ALL MY SHORT COMINGS AND DOWN FALL'S BUT THE TRUTH OF THIS MATTER THAT WOULD BE ANOTHER EPISODE TO CONTINUED ONLY GOD KNOWNS WHAT NEXT. OH YEAH! LET'S GET BACK TO WHAT I WAS EXPLAINING LOOK AT THE HOLY DIVINE POWER WORKING IN THIS VERY HOUR NOT BRAGGING MY THREE CHILDREN AND THREE GRAND-CHILDREN WHICH IS THE NEXT GENERATION SO HAPPEN TO GIVE GREAT PROPHECY, PREDICTIONS

AS WEATHER BROADCASTERS AND JOURNALIST I'M GRATEFUL FOR THIS SPECIAL ANOINTED GIFTED THAT IS HANDLED DOWN BY OUR HEAVENLY FATHER IT'S UP TO EVERY INDIVIDUAL CARRY THE MANTEL. HOWEVERY I PERSONALLY TAKE NOTHING FOR GRANTED NOR LIGHTLY BECAUSE I GREW UP NOT HAVING BOTH PARENTS AND NEITHER MY BOTH GRAND-PARENTS NEVERTHELESS MAY BE ALL OF MY PRAYER'S OR PREDICTIONS, PROPHECY WILL CONTINUE TO IMPACT THEIR LIVES AND OTHER'S AS WELL SO THEREFORE WHEN I'AM DEAD AND GONE THIS TORCH OR MANTEL WILL BE PASSED HOPEFULLY TO ALL GENERATIONS TO COME RATHER BOY, GIRL, MEN AND WOMEN.

WHAT DOES THE BIBLE MEAN OUT OF THE MOUTHS OF BABES? THE YOUNG; AND INNOCENT ARE OFTEN UNEXPECTEDLY WISE.

PSALMS 8:2 OUT OF THE MOUTH OF BABES AND SUCKLINGS HAST THOU ORDAINED STRENGTH BECAUSE OF THINE ENEMIES THAT THOU MIGHTEST STILL THE ENEMY AND THE AVENGER.

PHARAOH'S ARMY DESTROYED

PHARAOH'S ARMY WILL DROWN MOSES HAS PART THE RED SEA ONCE AGAIN MY ENEMIES SNEAKY, AMBUSHED EVIL ATTACKS MY CONTENDER'S AND RIVALRIES ON THIS PARTICULAR DAY OCTOBER 21, 2022 THESE DEMON'S TRYING TO SNATCH ME BACK INTO THEIR MERCURY MUDDY WATERS DEALING WITH HOUSE WHOLE BLOODLINE FRE-NEMY AND GENERATIONAL WITCHES, WARLOCKS PHARAOH'S HOUSE WHOLE UNDERCOVER EVIL DOERS WALKEN NAVIGATING WITH SUCH PURE HATERED, HARBORING, RESENTMENT BESIDES LURKING IN THE UNSEEN REALM OPERATING LIKE TWO HEADED SNAKES, DRAGON'S DEMON'S BIGFOOT DERANGED CRAZY BEARS THEY'RE MOST DEFINITELY, ABSOLUTELY GREAT PRETENDERS WHO HAS BEING EXPOSED AS SECRET IMPOSTERS AGENTS WHO IS WORKING FROM LUCIFER KINGDOM SYSTEM BEHIND SCENES. OH YEAH! LET'S REWIND THIS FILM I FORGOT TO MENTION THAT TWO WEEKS AGO PRIOR TO LEADING UP TO THIS ATTACK THE HOLY ANGELS CAME WITH A DIVINE DOWNLOAD REVELATION THERE WAS THIS GRIZZLY BLACK BEAR, AND A APE WALKING OR PERHAPS ROAMING IN THE STREETS NEVERTHELESS I PAUSED IMMEDIATELY CALLED ANIMAL CONTROL NEXT THING I WOKEUP FROM THAT VISION VERY STRANGE OR UNUSUAL ESPECIALLY WACKY AND BIZARRE OKAY MOVING FORWARD NOW GOD SAID THAT YOU ALREADY HAVE THE BLUE PRINT

OF THAT ROADMAP AND FORESIGHT TO STAND WITH SUPER POWER, ARMOR AND AUTHORITY MOREOVER THESE UNRESTED STUBBORN BULLIES PLOTS, SCHEMES COME TO ENSLAVED YOU BY KEEPING YOU UPUNDER THEIR WICKED EVIL DICTATORSHIP RULES WHO IS ACTUALLY OUT TO ANTAGONIZE BRINGING HELL CHAOS DISTRACTIONS AND FURTHERMORE OPERATING FROM A COMPETITIVE SPIRIT THEY ALL WAS TRYING TO ONE UP ME EVERYTIME WHO DOES THAT? OH YEAH! LET'S NOT FORGET THOSE GANGSTALKERS WHO RUB SALT IN TO THE WOUND, THEY MAKE THE UNPLEASANT SITUATION THAT YOU ARE IN EVEN WORSE OFTEN BY REMINDING YOU OF YOUR CURRENT OR PAST FAILURES AND FAULTS. I COME TO FOREWARN ALL MANKIND ON TODAY OF THIS NONESENSE DYSFUNCTIONAL BEHAVIOR SCARE TACTICS AMBIGUOUS INSULTING MAN'S CHARACTER, INTEGRITY NEVER ALLOW THESE TYPE OF IMPOSTERS TO RULE, JUDGE OR BE THE JURY AND PROSECUTOR OVER YOUR SOUL THE LORD SPOKE IN HIS WORD THAT HE WAS GOING TO SILENCE THE LION'S, ENEMIES MOUTH'S AND WHICH HE WILL BRING SHAME UPON THEM THAT WHOEVER MOCK AND TEASE BLASPHEME THE HOLY SPIRIT IT'S IN THE WORD ALSO SPEAKS DO NOT TOUCH MY ANOINTED ONES, AND DO MY PROPHETS NO HARM UNDERSTANDING THE DARK SIDE OF AN EMENY MINDS THEY SIMPLY ONLY CARE FOR THEMSELVES ONCE AGAIN BUT DEEPLY INSIDE THEY'RE SECRELY UPSET TERRIFIED SCREEMING OUT WITH LOW KEY FRUSTRATION FEELING OF BEING ANNOYED, ESPECIALLY BECAUSE THE LACK OF THEIR INABILITY TO CHANGE OR ACHIEVE SOMETHING WHICH YOU HAVE TOIL WORK HARD INTO THE FIELDS OVER FORTY PLUS YRS ONLY GOD KNOWN'S AND JUDGES MAN'S HEARTS SURVIVING CAPTIVITY ONLY TO REALIZE BY DISCRENING THESE DERANG, WACKY GRIZZLY BEAR'S

THEIR INTENTIONS IS TO COME ABUSE, PREY UPON AND INTIMIDATE BY WEAKENING BY GAINING POWER TO QUIET MY VOICE NOT ONLY THAT BUT TO DERANK MY POSITION FURTHEMORE THEY'RE TRYING AVERY EFFORTS ATTEMPED TO STEAL MY CROWN, INHERITANCE NO EVIL WILL PREVAILED SAYS THE LORD

"EXHIBITING LACK OF RESPECT RUDE AND DISCOURTEOUS"

THE ENEMIES ARE LOSING THEIR MIND TRYING TO KEEP UP WITH YOU, THEY'RE TOTALLY OUT OF ORDER BECAUSE THE LACK OF UNIVERSE LAWS BY DISHONORING, DISOBEDIENT AND DISRESPECTING.

WHAT IS REPROBATION? THE NATURAL PERSON DOES NOT ACCEPT THE THINGS OF THE SPIRIT OF GOD FOR THEY ARE FOLLY TO HIM AND HE IS NOT WELL PLEASED WITH THEIR FOOLISHNESS.

ROMANS 1:28 AND EVEN AS THEY DID NOT LIKE TO RETAIN GOD IN THEIR KNOWLEDGE, GOD GAVE THEM OVER TO A REPROBATE MIND, TO DO THOSE THINGS WHICH ARE NOT CONVENIENT.

HOW TO STAND UP TO SOMEONE WHO DOESN'T VALUE YOU?

1. DON'T JUSTIFY THEIR BEHAVIORS

2. DON'T LOSE YOURSELF

3. DON'T OVERCOMPENSATE

4. DON'T STAY FOR THE WRONG REASONS

5. DON'T STICK AROUND

6. IF YOU NEED TO STAND UP TO SOMEONE WHO DOESN'T VALUE YOU DO SO SOON!

"PHARAOH'S ARMY DESTROYED YOU WILL'NT SEE THEM NO MORE"

2 SAMUEL 22:31 AS FOR GOD, HIS WAY IS PERFECT: THE LORD'S WORD IS FLAWLESS; HE SHIELDS ALL WHO TAKE REFUGE IN HIM.

THIS MY EXODUS MOMENT

END

REJECTED BY KINSMEN FOR HONORING MY GOD'S GIVEN GIFT'S AND SPIRITUAL GROWTH.

CAN YOU LITERALLY IMAGINE PEOPLE THINK YOU'RE STUPID, DUMB BLIND AND IGNORANT THEY THOUGHT THAT YOU WERE GOING TO STAY STUCK IN THEIR YARD OF FOOLISHNESS, CONSEQUENCES BY THEIR ACTIONS, BEING STUPIDITY ONLY TO LEAVE YOU HOLDING THEIR BAG OF MESS I DON'T THINK SO WHEN IN FACT YOU CAME TO HELP SERVE THEM AND FAMILY. NOW IT'S YOUR TIME TO PICK UP YOUR MATE MOVE FORWARDS INTO YOUR CALL OF DIVINE DESTINY NOW ALL OF SUDDENT THEY WANT TO TURN UP ON YOU TO THROW SHADE ON YOU ONLY TO BE INSULTED AND ABUSED BY PUTTING STUMBLING STONES, ROADBLOCK'S WHO DOES THAT? SUCH SILLY RABBIT'S TRICKS ARE FOR KIDS YOU GUYS CAN'T CATCH ME I MOVE ONE STEP AHEAD OF MY ENEMIES INTO THE SUPERSECRET NATURAL REALM

THE GAME OF THRONE'S TACTICS OVER YOUR TIME IS UP GOD HAS EXPOSED EACH AND EVERYONE OF YOUR SECRETLY SKILLFUL ACTS OF CUNNING SCHEMES PLOTS.

"HAIL MIXED WITH FIRE"

A VALUABLE LESSION TO LEARN FROM THE KING'S DAUGHTER DEMONSTRATING WALKEN IN LOVE

PEOPLE NEED TO LEARN HOW TO VALUE RESPECT OTHER PEOPLE'S TIME NEVER TAKE IT FOR GRANTED

ESPECIALLY WHEN GOD HAS SENT FORTH ONE OF HIS FAITHFUL CIA SECRET AGENTS BE EXTREMELY CAREFUL HOW YOU MISHANDLED THE KING'S CHILD

THESE PEOPLE WANTED TO BRING SHAME BUT MY ALMIGHTY ABBA FATHER WILL REVERSEBACK TO THE SENDER'S AND WILL BRING DOUBLE BLESSING, HONOR'S. TO THOSE WHO WILL STAY HUMBLE, FAITHFUL AND MEEKNESS TO THE CALL WE AS BELIEVER'S MUST ALWAYS REMEMBER EVERY LESSION OR TEST IS ONLY SETTING YOU UP FOR A HIGHER-RANKING POSITION TO LEVEL UP FOR YOUR KINGDOM RULERSHIP PROMOTION, CELEBRATIONS.

"A STUBBORN REBELLION LOST GENERATION"

"A WISE MAN FEARETH GOD WALK WITH THE WISE"

PROVERBS 14:24 THE CROWN OF THE WISE IS THEIR RICHES: BUT THE FOOLISHNESS OF FOOLS IS FOLLY.

14:25 A TRUE WITNESS DELIVERETH SOULS: BUT A DECEITFUL WITNESS SPEAKETH LIES.

PROVERBS 14:30 A SOUND HEART IS THE LIFE OF THE FLESH: BUT ENVY THE ROTTNNESS OF THE BONES.

PROVERBS 14:31 HE THAT OPPRESSETH THE POOR REPROACETH HIS MAKER: BUT HE THAT HONOURETH HIM HATH MERCY ON THE POOR.

ROMANS 16:17 I APPEAL TO YOU, BROTHERS, TO WATCH OUT FOR THOSE WHO CAUSE DIVISION, AND CREAT OBSTACLES CONTRAY TO THE DOCTRINE THAT YOU HAVE BEEN TAUGHT; AVOID THEM.

"MAN-HOOD JOURNEY"

TO PRAY WITHOUT CEASING TO HAVE OUR MINDS ALWAYS'S ON THE THINGS OF GOD, TO BE IN CONSTANT COMMUNICATION WITH HIM, SO THAT EVERY MOMENT MAY BE AS FRUITFUL AS POSSIBLE

1 THESSALONIANS 5:16 REJOICE ALWAYS, PRAY WITH OUT CEASING GIVE THANKS IN ALL CIRCUMATANCES; FOR THIS IS THE WILL OF GOD IN CHRIST JESUS FOR YOU.

"THE RIGHTEOUS LIPS SPEAKS PEACE"

PROVERBS 16:13 RIGHTEOUS LIPS ARE THE DELIGHT OF KINGS: AND THEY LOVE HIM THAT SPEAKETH RIGHT.

16:24 PLEASANT WORDS ARE AS AN HONEYCOMB, SWEET TO THE SOUL, AND HEALTH TO THE BONES.

16:27 AN UNGODLY MAN DIGGETH UP EVIL: AND IN HIS LIPS THERE IS AS A BURNING FIRE.

SEEKING GOD'S WISDOM
IN PERILOUS TIME'S

ON THIS PARTICULAR DAY OCTOBER 29, 2022 I WAS SUPPOSED TO ATTENED THIS SPECIAL EVENT THE OCCASION PREHAPS WAS BRUNCH I PAID FOR THE TICKET IN ADVANCE MOREOVER WEEKS IN ADVANCE PRIOR LEADING UP TO THIS MOMENT BY THE SUPER-POWER OF THE HOLY GHOST DROP A SUPER-NATURAL DIVINE DOWNLOAD REVELATION INTO MY INNER INTUITION MAN HIS EXACT WORD'S DON'T GO WOW! WARNING ALERT DISCERNING WITH CAUTIONS HOWEVER IMMEDIATELY I SURRENDER OBEYED AND COMPLY WITH HIS COMMAND. MY STEPS ARE ORDER TESTING THE FRUIT OF THE SPIRITS WALKEN IN THE SPIRIT OBEYING THE HOLY SPIRIT DINNING OUT WITH MY FRENEMIES. STAY TUNE THIS EPISODE TO BE CONTINUED Pt. 1

BREAKING NEW'S ALERT Pt. 2 THREE DAY'S LATER ON OCTOBER 31, 2022 I'VE RECEIVED A POWERFUL PROPHETIC REVELATION FROM ANOTHER GREAT PROPHETESS HER EXACT WORD'S WAS YOU TOOK HEED BY HEARKENING OBEYING GOD'S COMMAND NOT TO GO SIT AT THE FRENEMIES TABLE LISTEN FURTHERMORE SHE MENTION THAT GOD WAS VERY PLEASED AND I DODGED THE BULLETS BY NOT ATTENDING THAT EVENT THEY WERE SURPRISED EXTREMELY OUTRAGE ANGER SHOCK THEM.

THEIR FINAL TAKEDOWN BACKFIRE MISSION WAS NOT ACCOMPLISHED THESE GANGSTALKER'S ALSO FAILED TO REALIZE GOD IS OMNIPOTENCE, OMNISCIENCE, AND OMNIPRESENCE I'VE REVERSED THAT CURSE OF WITCHCRAFT BY A NO SHOW THESE LOW VIBRATION INDIVIDUALS CALL THEMSELVES LOVING JESUS CHRIST AND HATING THEIR FELLOW NEIGHBOR'S WHO DOES THAT? THIS TYPE OF DISORDER CONFUSION BEHAVIOR RUNNING RAMPANT THROUGH OUR WORLD OF SOCIETY TODAY I'M CURIOUS EAGER TO KNOW THEY TRULY THOUGHT THAT THEY WHERE GOING TO PRACTICE SUCH EVIL BLOOD SACRIFICE RITUAL CASTING MAGIC AND SPELLS ON THE GOLDEN CHILD OF THE MOST HIGH WHO BELIEVED TO BE VULNERABLE TO A FORMED OF WITCHCRAFT JEALOUSY NEIGHBORS SUCH FOOLISHNESS BEHAVIOR MOCKERY EXCUSE ME FOR A BRIEF MOMENT HERE THEY'RE ACTING OPERATING LIKE A LOONEY TUNE SYNDROME DISPLAYING, MENTAL DISORDERS SILLY RABBITS TRICKS ARE FOR KIDS PEOPLE ACTIONS ACTUALLY DEMONSTRATE OR EXHIBIT THEIR TRUE COLORS AND CHARACTERISTIC TRAITS IT SHOW'S YOUR MOTIVES EITHER PURE GOOD OR EVIL INTENTIONS I EARNESTLY THANK MY HEAVENLY FATHER FOR HIDDEN ME IN HIS SECRET PLACE THE WOLVES ARE OUT TO CAPTURE THE SHEEP ONLY TO LEAD THEM FOR THE SLAUGHTER WOW! IT'S AMAZING PRETTY IMPRESSIVE MOVING IN SLIENCE HEARING THE VOICE OF GOD FOR SUCH A TIME AS THIS.

"HALLELUJAH PEACE BE STILL IN THE MIST OF ALL CHAOS"

"DINNING OUT WITH YOUR FRENEMIES"

PROVERBS 3:25 BE NOT AFRAID OF SUDDEN FEAR, NEITHER OF THE DESOLATION OF THE WICKED, WHEN IT COMETH.

PROVERBS 15:13 A MERRY HEART MAKETH A CHEERFUL COUNTENANCE: BUT BY SORROW OF THE HEART THE SPIRIT IS BROKEN.

15:14 THE HEART OF HIM THAT HATH UNDERSTANDING SEEKETH KNOWLEDGE: BUT THE MOUTH OF FOOLS FEEDETH ON FOOLISHNESS.

15:15 ALL THE DAYS OF THE AFFLICTED ARE EVIL: BUT HE THAT IS OF A MERRY HEART HATH A CONTINUAL FEAST.

15:17 BETTER IS A DINNER OF HERBS WHERE LOVE IS, THAN A STALLED OX AND HATRED THERE WITH.

15:18 A WRATHFUL MAN STIRRETH UP STRIFE: BUT HE THAT IS SLOW TO ANGER APPEASETH STRIFE.

2 CORINTHIANS 2:11 LEST SA'TAN SHOULD GET AN ADVANTAGE OF US: FOR WE ARE NOT IGNORANT OF HIS DEVISE.

"LISTEN TO A PARABLE"

"YOU EITHER FOR ME OR AGAINST ME"

1 JOHN 4:1 BELOVED, BELIEVE NOT EVERY SPIRIT, BUT TRY THE SPIRITS WHETHER THEY ARE OF GOD: BECAUSE MANY FALSE PROPHETS ARE GONE OUT INTO THE WORLD.

1 JOHN 4:3 AND EVERY SPIRIT THAT CONFESSETH NOT THAT JESUS CHRIST IS COME IN THE FLESH IS NOT OF GOD: AND THIS IS THAT SPIRIT OF ANTICHRIST, WHERE OF YE HAVE HEARD THAT IT SHOULD COME; AND EVEN NOW ALLREADY IS IT IN THE WORLD.

"MAN'S FIGHTING HIS OWN MIND, HEART INTERNAL AFFLICTIONS AND RUMOR OF WAR'S"

OH! LORD MY REDEEMER I'AM CRYING OUT ON THE BEHALF OF MY GENERATION AND GENERATIONS TO COME HELP US TO GAIN A SENSE OF MORAL LIFE VICTORY BY RECOVERYING REPAIRING OUR SICK LOST MINDS WITH A BROKEN SPIRIT AND CONTRITE HEART THAT WE COME HUMBLY BEFORE YOU GOD ACKNOWLEDGING OUR SIN AND PROCLAIMING GOD'S GOODNESS IN THIS FINAL HOUR.

"WE'RE DEFINITLEY EXPERIENCING AND LIVING IN BIBLICAL PROPHECIES END TIME'S"

ROMANS 7:23 BUT I SEE ANOTHER LAW IN MY MEMBERS, WARRING AGAINST THE LAW OF MY MIND, AND BRINGING ME INTO CAPTIVITY TO THE LAW OF SIN WHICH IS IN MY MEMBERS.

"THIS WORLD NEED'S A BREAKTHROUGH"

SYNCHRONICITY NUMEROLOGY BIBLICAL PROPHECIES

SIGNS SYMBOLS AND WONDER'S ON THIS DIVINE UNIQUE SPECIAL DAY OF NOVEMBER 11,2022 LET'S DIVE INTO THIS MESSAGE HOWEVER I WAS ON THE PHONE COMMUINCATING PERHAPS WITH A BUSINESS PARTNER BRIEFLY AND WE STARTED TO RAP UP THE CONVERTSATION NEXT THING SHE MENTION HER PHONE EXTENTION WHICH SO HAPPEN TO BE THE NUMBER 111 I STOP AND PAUSE FOR A SECOND THEN STARTED EXPLAINING TO HER WHAT THOSE NUMBERS MEAN BIBLICALLY HEAVEN'S GATES ARE OPENING IN THIS ELEVENTH HOUR IN TIME HISTORY FOR SOME PEOPLE LET'S BREAK THIS DOWN BY WAYS OF INTERPRETING, EXPLAINING THIS INFORMATION BASED UPON THE MEANING OF 11:11.

1. EVERYTHING IN ALIGNMENT FOR GREAT THINGS TO ENTER INTO YOUR LIFE.

2. BREAKDOWNS AWAKENING FROM YOUR DEEP SLEEP.

3. IT'S A NEW WORLD NEW DOORS OPENING WITH GREAT OPPORTUNITY.

4. BEING GUIDED PROTECTED BY HOLY ANGEL'S KEEP WALKEN BY FAITH YOUR DEFINITLEY ON THE RIGHT PATH.

5. DIVINE CONNECTIONS NOTHING IS RANDOM.

6. SYNCHRONICITY-HIDDEN MEANINGS.

7. SYMBOLIC SECRET CODE'S LEANING TOWARD GOD'S UNDERSTANDING NOT MAN'S WAYS.

8. ENDING BREAKING OLD HABITS, CYCLES, AND PATTERNS.

9. IT'S TIME TO RECEIVE YOUR DOUBLE PORTION.

10. DON'T FORGET TO PROTECT YOUR MIND BY PUTTING ON THE HELMET OF SALVATION AND ALWAYS GUARD YOUR HEART WITH THE BREASTPLATE OF RIGHTEOUSNESS.

11. WALKEN IN LOVE, PEACE WITH A HIGH FREQUENCY VIBRATION ANTICIPATING FOR AN AMAZING NEW EXCITING LIFE ADVENTURES THAT AWAIT YOU.

"LISTEN TO A PARABLE"

DEUTERONOMY 1:11 MAY THE LORD, THE GOD OF YOUR FATHERS, MAKE YOU A THOUSAND TIMES AS MANY AS YOU ARE AND BLESS YOU, AS HE HAS PROMISED YOU!

HEBREWS 11:1 NOW FAITH IS THE SUBSTANCE OF THINGS HOPED FOR, THE EVIDENCE OF THINGS NOT SEEN.

THERE'S DEEP IMPARTATION FROM THE MOUTH OF A PROPHET

ON THIS DAY OF NOVEMBER 19,2022 SUDDENLY I RECEIVED A CALL FROM THE MAN OF GOD PASTOR NELSON DISCRENING WEALTH TRANS-FER HE SEES INTO THE WORLD OF SUPERNATURAL WHAT'S TAKEN PLACE WERE GOD'S HANDS DEMONSTRATING DISPLAYING MIRACULOUS SIGNS, WONDERS WITH DOUBLE PORTION OF INCREASES AND BLESSING UPON MY LIFE STAY TUNE THIS EPOSIDE TO BE CONTINUED Pt. 1

BREAKING NEW'S REPORT Pt. 2 ONE DAY LATER ON THIS NIGHT BETWEEN THE HOURES 3:00 am EARLY MORNING NOVEMBER 20,2022 I'VE RECEIVED ANOTHER AMAZING DIVINE PROPHETIC DREAM DOWNLOAD REVELATION FROM OUR HEAVENLY FATHER IN ADDITION TO THIS ENCOUNTER MYSELF AND TWO OTHER INDIVIDUALS WHERE INSIDE A CLOTHING STORE SHOPPING MOREOVER THE HOLY SPIRIT STARTED REVEALING TO ME SOME ROYALITY CHECKS WHICH I'VE RECEIVED FROM AROUND THE FOUR CORNERS OF EARTH. SUDDENLY HOWEVER I WOKE UP EMBRACING CONVEYING THE MESSAGE RECEIVING BELIEVING WALKING BY FAITH THAT WHICH NEVERTHELESS THIS CONFIRMATION WAS BASED UPON TWO INDIVIDUALS COME TO TOUCH IN AGREEMENT ON

EARTH IN A DREAM FOR INSTANCE A VISION AT NIGHT OH! HE WALKS WITH US THE VOICE I HEAR FALLEN UPON MAN'S EAR'S GIVEN INSTURCTION FROM MAN'S BED POST TO EITHER BELIEVE OR NOT TO BELIEVE REMEMBER WE WALK BY FAITH NOT BY SIGHT. WRITE YOUR VISIONS IRON SHARPENS IRON

UNLEST TWO WALK IN AGREEMENT TO SHOW GOD'S SUPERPOWER GLORY AND MANIFESTING INTO THE LIVES OF A FAITHFUL FOLLOWER AND BELIEVER.

"HEAVEN GATE'S ARE OPEN"

AMOS 3:3 CAN TWO WALK TOGETHER, EXCEPT THEY BE AGREED?

ECCLESIASTES 4:9 TWO ARE BETTER THAN ONE; BECAUSE THEY HAVE A GOOD REWARD OF THEIR LABOUR.

MATTHEW 18:19 AGAIN I SAY UNTO YOU, THAT IF TWO OF YOU AGREE ON EARTH AS TOUCHING ANY THING THAT THEY SHALL ASK, IT SHALL BE DONE FOR THEM OF MY FATHER WHICH IS IN HEAVEN.

"HEARKEN TO THE VOICE OF GOD"

ANOTHER GENERATION CARRYING THE REVELATION

LUKE 1:14 AND THOU SHALT HAVE JOY AND GLADNESS; AND MANY SHALT REJOICE AT HIS BIRTH.

LUKE 1:15 FOR HE SHALL BE GREAT IN THE SIGHT OF THE LORD AND SHALL DRINK NEITHER WINE NOR STRONG DRINK; AND HE SHALL BE FILLED WITH THE HOLY GHOST, EVEN FROM HIS MOTHER WOMB.

LUKE 1:16 AND MANY OF THE CHILDERN OF ISRAEL SHALL HE TURN TO THE LORD THEIR GOD.

LUKE 1:17 AND HE SHALL GO BEFORE HIM IN THE SPIRIT AND POWER OF ELIAS, TO TURN THE HEARTS OF THE FATHERS TO THE CHILDREN, AND THE DISOBEDIENT TO THE WISDOM OF THE JUST; TO MAKE READY A PEOPLE PREPARED FOR THE LORD.

LUKE 1:26 AND IN THE SIXTH MONTH THE ANGEL GABRIEL WAS SENT FROM GOD UNTO A CITY OF GALILEE, NAMED NAZARETH,

LUKE 1:27 TO A VIRGIN ESPOUSED TO A MAN WHOSE NAME WAS JOSEPH, OF THE HOUSE OF DAVID; AND THE VIRGIN'S NAME WAS MARY.

LUKE 1:28 AND THE ANGEL CAME IN UNTO HER, AND SAID, HAIL, THOU THAT ART HIGHLY FAVOURED, THE LORD IS WITH THEE: BLESSED ART THOU AMONG WOMEN.

LUKE 1:29 AND WHEN SHE SAW HIM, SHE WAS TROUBLED AT HIS SAYING, AND CAST IN HER MIND WHAT MANNER OF SALUTATION THIS SHOULD BE.

LUKE 1:30 AND THE ANGEL SAID UNTO HER, FEAR NOT, MARY: FOR THOU HAST FOUND FAVOUR WITH GOD.

LUKE 1:31 AND, BEHOLD, THOU SHALT CONCEIVE IN THY WOMB, AND BRING FORTH A SON, AND SHALT CALL HIS NAME JESUS.

"ANOTHER STAR IS BORN"

LUKE 1:32 HE SHALL BE GREAT, AND SHALL BE CALLED THE SON OF THE HIGHEST: AND THE LORD GOD SHALL GIVE UNTO HIM THE THRONE OF HIS FATHER DAVID:

LUKE 1:33 AND HE SHALL REIGN OVER THE HOUSE OF JACOB FOR EVER; AND OF HIS KINGDOM THERE SHALL BE NO END.

LUKE 1:34 THEN SAID MARY UNTO THE ANGEL, HOW SHALL THIS BE, SEEING I KNOW NOT A MAN?

LUKE 1:35 AND THE ANGEL ANSWERED AND SAID UNTO HER, THE HOLY GHOST SHALL COME UPON THEE: THEREFORE ALSO THAT HOLY THING WHICH SHALL BE BORN OF THEE SHALL BE CALLED THE SON OF GOD.

"HE SHALL BE CALLED WONDERFUL COUNSELOR PRINCE OF PEACE"

LUKE 1:45 AND BLESSED IS SHE THAT BELIEVED: FOR THERE SHALL BE A PERFORMANCE OF THOSE THINGS WHICH WERE TOLD HER FROM THE LORD.

LUKE 1:50 AND HIS MERCY IS ON THEM THAT FEAR HIM FROM GENERATION TO GENERATION

LUKE 1:51 HE HATH SHEWED STRENGTH WITH HIS ARM; HE HAT SCATTERED THE PROUD IN THE IMAGINATION OF THEIR HEARTS.

LUKE 1:70 AS HE SPAKE BY THE MOUTH OF HIS HOLY PROPHETS, WHICH HAVE BEEN SINCE THE WORLD BEGAN:

LUKE 1:71 THAT WE SHOULD BE SAVED FROM OUR ENEMIES, AND FROM THE HAND OF ALL THAT HATE US;

LUKE 1:72 TO PERFORM THE MERCY PROMISED TO OUR FATHERS, AND TO REMEMBER HIS HOLY COVENANT;

LUKE 1:73 THE OATH WHICH HE SWARE TO OUR FATHER ABRAHAM,

LUKE 1:74 THAT HE WOULD GRANT UNTO US, THAT WE BEING DELIVERED OUT OF THE HAND OF OUR ENEMIES MIGHT SERVE HIM WITH OUT FEAR,

LUKE 1:75 IN HOLINESS AND RIGHTEOUSNESS BEFORE HIM, ALL THE DAYS OF OUR LIFE.

LUKE 1:76 AND THOU, CHILD SHALT BE CALLED THE PROPHET OF THE HIGHEST: FOR THOU SHALT GO BEFORE THE FACE OF THE LORD TO PREPARE HIS WAY;

"HE SHALL RULE AND REIGN OVER MANY NATIONS"

LUKE 1:77 TO GIVE KNOWLEDGE OF SAVATION UNTO HIS PEPOLE BE THE REMISSION OF THEIR SINS,

LUKE 1:78 THROUGH THE TENDER MERCY OF OUR GOD; WHERE BY THE DAY SPRING FROM ON HIGH HATH VISITED US,

"TAKE HEED LISTEN TO A PARABLE"

LUKE 1:79 TO GIVE LIGHT TO THEM THAT SIT IN DARKNESS AND IN THE SHADOW OF DEATH, TO GUIDE OUR FEET INTO THE WAY OF PEACE.

LIKE 1:80 AND THE CHILD GREW, AND WAXED STRONG IN SPIRIT, AND WAS IN THE DESERTS TILL THE DAY OF HIS SHEWING UNTO ISRAEL.

"THOU CHILD SHALT BE CALLED THE PROPHET OF THE HIGHEST IT'S ONLY GOD THAT ORDAINS A PROPHET"

ARE YOU A WORLD CHANGER?

ACKNOWLEDGMENTS

LET'S BEGIN WITH GIVEN HONORS PRAISE WORSHIP AND GLORY TO OUR KING OF KINGS FOR SAVING A SINNER LIKE ME, REDEEMING MY SOUL FROM THE PIT OF HELL AND DYING UPON MY OWN SWORD MOREOVER YAHWEH, YESHUA LOVE'S ALL MANKIND

IN ADDITION I'M GRATEFUL, HONORED TO HAVE SUCH PRIVILEGE AND OPPORTUNITY NEVERTHELESS, BY CARRYING THIS MANTEL OF THE SUPERNATURAL MIRACULOUS PROPHETIC POWERFUL ANOINTING GIFT.

FURTHERMORE, GOD HAS LEAD, APPOINTED MY STEPS FOR SUCH A TIME AS THIS TO COME AND PARTAKE AS A WITNESS EXPERIENCING WITH THE CONTACTS OF INVISIBLE, TANGIBLE DEMONSTRATIONS DISPLAYING MANY DREAMS AND VISIONS ALONG THIS REMARKABLE AMAZING POWERFUL MYSTERIOUS MYSTERY PATH CALLED DESTINY

LAST BUT NOT LEASE OH YEAH! I'VE FORGOT TO MENTION THANKS TO EVERYONE WHO HATE ME AND DESPISE ME AND WENT UP AGAINST MY FATHER AND I Y'ALL TRIED EVERY TRICK EVIL, WICKED SPELL TRAPS ILL WILL INTENTION OR DESIRE PLOTS AND ALL MALICE ATTEMPS

NO WEAPON THAT FORMED AGAINST ME SHALL PROSPER
THE BLOOD STILL WORKS

THANK YOU TO ALL WHO SUPPORTED ME IN THE PAST
AND IN THE PRESENT. I AM INDEBTED TO YOU FROM THE
BOTTOM OF MY HEART WITH GREAT SINCERITY MAY
GOD'S PEACE REST UPON YOU AND MAY EACH ONE OF
Y'ALL UNDERSTAND GOD'S GIFT AND WILL THROUGH
LIFE UNCERTAIN ARDUOUS SPIRITUAL SUPERNATURAL
BATTLES.

LUKE 4:18 THE SPIRIT OF THE LORD IS UPON ME, BECAUSE
HE HATH ANOINTED ME TO PREACH THE GOSPEL TO
THE POOR; HE HATH SENT ME TO HEAL THE BROKEN
HEARTED, TO PREACH DELIVERANCE TO THE CAPTIVES,
AND RECOVERING OF SIGHT TO THE BLIND, TO SET AT
LIBERTY THEM THAT ARE BRUISED.

A BENDICTION

NUMBERS 6:24-25-26-27
6:24 THE LORD BLESS THEE, AND KEEP THEE:

6:25 THE LORD MAKE HIS FACE SHINE UPON THEE, AND BE GRACIOUS UNTO THEE.

6:26 THE LORD LIFT UP HIS COUNTENCE UPON THEE. AND GIVE THEE PEACE:

6:27 AND THEY SHALL PUT MY NAME UPON THE CHILDREN OF ISRAEL; AND I WILL BLESS THEM.

ABOUT THE AUTHOR

Jennifer Denise Thomas was born on June 29,1966 in Los Angeles, California. She accepted Jesus Christ as her Lord and Savior at the tender age of thirteen, Jennifer is a visionary. She has the gift of revelation and the spirit of discernment. She recalls having dreams and night visitations at the tender age of four and then growing into adulthood and watching those dreams and visions come to full fruition, Jennifer has found grace, mercy, truth peace, understanding, and love within the body of Christ. As a foster youth, she faced adversity: emotional and financial hardship, abuse, neglect; and rejection. Nevertheless, she was able to overcome each obstacle, she rose from the ashes of defeat and a place of darkness and despair by grounding herself in faith. Jennifer has served in the work force and in the Community for nearly forty years as a Customer Service Associate, motor coach operator, a semi-trailer truck operator and she went on to become a taxicab driver. She truly has a giving heart and a Charitable spirit, for she gives her time, energy, and guidance to various women's shelters, plus she has countless hours working behind the scenes on political campaigns; and She has provided shelter, food and clothing to those who are in need for over forty years. She is a mother of three biological children; however, she has provided love and care for many. Jennifer is currently ministering to those in the convalescent homes. She is also participating on a project with the Union Rescue Mission on skid row. This project addresses the homelessness crisis that has Impacted people around the Globe. Jennifer has a passion for helping others find their destiny in life. It's her life's mission to teach other's that God has a plan and a purpose for their life. Finally, Jennifer's current endeavors include fashion design, writing more books producing audio books and also adapting her projects into films and TV series she's mentoring young men and women, not only is she providing assistance or care for the disable/elderly, Jennifer, has also worn many hats. Last but not lease, she sat in class of Hebrew Institute of Theological studies. Her instructor was one of our world leaders, Dr. Michelle Corral, she goes to rallies for peace and justice, stopping violence, and increasing minimum wages. She stood with many more great world leaders such as Nation Action Network Rev. AL Sharpton and Pastor K.W. Tuloss. Jennifer is truly a Modern-day Samaritan Humanitarian/Philanthropist.